# SnowStorm King

H. L. Macfarlane

# COPYRIGHT



ISBN-13: 978-1-9160163-3-0

Published by Macfarlane Lantern Publishing, 2020

Glasgow, Scotland

As with Chronicles of Curses book one, this one's for me.

# Prologue

Rumour had it there was a magician staying in Alder for winter. He was from far to the south, where snow never fell. Everyone wondered why someone so used to warm seas and balmy winds would ever wish to stay up in the mountains in the middle of December, when Alder was largely cut off from the rest of the world.

This winter was particularly bad – the worst the mountain town had seen in generations, if the elderly were to be believed. Supplies were running low, and the winds kept destroying doors and windows and roofs. Food was scarce, and people were starving. The king was at a loss for what to do; he couldn't help his subjects even as the days of endless night drew themselves like a blanket across the town. It seemed like nobody would survive long enough to see the sun again.

And yet the mysterious man from the south had somehow made it up to Alder, despite the treacherous, ice-covered paths and the ever-present risk of an avalanche swallowing travellers whole at any given moment. He sought refuge with a tailor and his family, who had been clothing the town in their warmest fabrics at their own expense.

They'd have no business left if everyone died, after all.

The tailor had a daughter - a talented young woman named Lily who was destined to take over her father's shop. He'd had more than a few betrothal requests since she came of age, but he was determined to only accept a perfect offer for his precious daughter.

Lily had other ideas. She was bored of Alder and its people who all looked the same: blonde hair that flashed gold in sunlight and silver in moonlight; skin as pale as the snow that blustered around them; eyes so blue they put the summer sky to shame. She craved something different.

For this reason alone her father never should have allowed the magician to stay under his roof. Lily was fascinated by his olive skin, tightly curled, dusky brown hair, and hazel eyes. They were like nothing she'd ever seen before. She spent the long hours of winter showing the man how to sew, and embroider, and work with difficult fabrics. In turn he sneaked into her bed at night, whispering tales of other lands, of different people, and of magic.

When the magician was called to the king's castle the people of Alder were suspicious and desperate in equal measure. They feared magic - most all common folk did - but if the mysterious man could bring an end to the deadly winter slowly leeching the life from them then so be it. They could deal with *one* instance of magic in return for their lives.

Lily didn't see the magician again after he visited the king. Some say he was murdered. Some say he merely went on his way, leaving Alder the same way he must have entered it – using a spell. She was heartbroken. But the rest of the town rejoiced, for the storms that plagued the mountainside finally abated. That year spring arrived early, and would continue to arrive early for the following twenty years of the king's prosperous reign.

But Lily's encounter with the magician was not so fortunate. By the time summer arrived she could no longer hide her swollen belly from the people of Alder. Everyone wondered who she had fallen into bed with, for Lily said nothing about him, even to her parents.

When the babe was born that autumn it became obvious. The little girl had soft, tawny hair, reminiscent of the owls that hunted in the forest. Her eyes were as dark as pine needles, and her skin appeared kissed by the sun even though she'd never been beneath its rays.

Lily's parents didn't know what to do. They had no other children – Lily was their only, beloved daughter. They could not reject her, nor the baby she clutched to her chest protectively. They were a family.

So though the townspeople shunned the child, and Lily's marriage proposals ran dry, the tailor and his family continued to live a respectable life in Alder. For people always needed new clothes, and their clothes were the best. They had even sewn clothes for the king's two young sons, though the youngest was rumoured to be so tempestuous that he set the clothes alight after receiving them.

Lily's parents passed away before her child turned ten, leaving her to run the family shop alone. She never married, and was never foolish enough to fall into bed with another man who whispered sweet nothings into her ear again. She stopped dreaming of lands where the sun was warm, the days ever-lasting and the people were kind instead of cruel.

No. Those dreams were inherited by her daughter, Elina.

# Chapter One

***Elina***

It didn't matter how inevitable the snow was every winter; Elina was always surprised when the first flakes fell. She hated the snow. She hated it down to her very core, and this year more than most.

For this winter was the worst anybody had experienced in twenty years. Elina might have thought this an exaggeration, had she not just turned twenty herself. She had lived through each and every one of those winters and could attest to the fact that this one, by far and away, was the worst.

Some said it was because the king had died, leaving his youngest son to take over the throne. Everyone had wanted the elder son, Gabriel, to inherit, but Gabriel was at war protecting their country from foreign invaders. So that left his younger brother sitting on the throne until he returned – something nobody wanted.

Kilian Hale had developed a bad reputation as he'd grown and it had only gotten worse when he reached adulthood. That was what everyone said, at least. It wasn't as if Elina had ever met her new king...not that she wanted to, anyway. But she was no stranger to rumours, and the rumours surrounding the younger Hale brother were even more prevalent than the ones surrounding Elina.

A playboy. A drunk. A terrible temper. Prone to disappearing for days on end on some hedonistic, self-serving quest. In truth Elina envied this – the prince could go wherever he wanted and do whatever he wanted no matter what people said about him.

But now that prince was regent and he could no longer leave the mountainside on a whim. Not that he could have with the winter weather having hit Alder so viciously, of course. The snowstorms that plagued the area had already half-buried the town, and the paths leading down the mountain were death traps. The road leading to the castle itself was only just barely kept clear because of the forest that enveloped the twisting path, but the boughs of the dark, foreboding trees were growing heavy. Eventually they would be able to hold onto the snow no longer, and the road to the castle would be cut off, too.

"Are you sure you don't want me to come with you, Elina?" her mother, Lily, coughed. They'd closed their shop early for the day, as the town was holding a meeting about the bad weather. Supplies were beginning to run low so, as a collective, they needed to decide how Alder was going to get through the winter.

"Of course not, mama," Elina soothed, brushing her mother's hair out of her face and readjusting her blanket. Lily had been sick for a few weeks now, though apparently it was nothing she couldn't handle. Elina wasn't convinced. Though her mother was still one year shy of forty, and retained her elegant good looks that had been the talk of the town once upon a time, she had grown decidedly frail. The mild winters of years gone by ensured that she had never *truly* gotten sick, but this year was different.

"You can't go to the town hall all by yourself, Elina," her mother protested. "You know what they're like. They'll –"

"It's nothing I cannot handle," she smiled. "And besides, it's on their own heads if they ignore me. They need us to keep making blankets and jackets and leggings and gloves, and for that we need materials. They can't possibly snub me at the meeting."

Lily looked unconvinced. The town had only gotten worse in their treatment of her daughter since her own parents died. It didn't seem to matter how obedient or talented Elina was – her tawny hair, forest-coloured eyes and eternally sun-kissed skin marked her for what she was. The daughter of an outsider. A strange man. A magician.

Though some people didn't really believe the foreigner from twenty years ago had been blessed with magic, Lily knew the truth. For how could she not? But she had never spoken much about the man to Elina, in part because it pained her to talk of him and in part to save her from knowing just how shameful her mother had been.

But Elina wasn't deaf. She wasn't blind. She wasn't stupid. She heard what the townspeople of Alder said, and she saw how they looked at her. She knew she was different, and for that she was hated. But she loved her mother fiercely, so not once did she ever consider blaming her for the way she was treated.

Elina kissed her mother on the forehead then wrapped herself up in her favourite blue cloak, made of fine, soft material that matched her dress. She pulled up the hood. "I won't be long, mama," she said as she opened the door, letting a blast of bitterly cold air through that had her wincing immediately. "I love you."

"You too, Elina."

The town hall wasn't far from the Brodeur tailor shop. If the ground hadn't been covered in a layer of thick, grey ice Elina would have reached her destination in under five minutes. But it *was* covered in ice, and Elina was always wary of walking on it in case she tripped and broke her neck, so by the time she reached the town hall the meeting had already started.

When she crept into the hall and tried to hide in the shadows at the back of the room a hundred eyes followed her.

*Oh, wonderful,* she thought. *I haven't even* said *anything and already I'm in the wrong.*

But to her relief nobody commented on her lateness. Apart from the occasional glare here and there Elina was ignored as the town head, Frederick, continued with his speech, for which Elina was grateful.

"It's not simply a case of rationing what we already have," Frederick said. "This winter seems set to last far longer than any winter we've had in twenty years. At this rate we won't make it past the end of January."

"This is all because the king died!" someone called out. "He had that magic from the foreigner, but it must have gone to the grave with him. We're all doomed!"

Several pairs of eyes darted towards Elina. She ignored them. She knew this story by heart: her father had been a magician who, after impregnating her mother and bestowing the gift of magic to the king, disappeared forever. She never understood how the king could be so revered for this supposed deal whilst Elina's mother was scorned for bearing the magician's child. The double standard would have made her laugh, if it hadn't made her life so bitterly lonely.

"Let's not base our current situation on rumours and suspicion," Frederick said, ever the diplomat. "We need a solid plan to get us through –"

"Isn't there that travelling couple staying in Gill's tavern?" someone else interrupted. "You know the two. The woman's a healer, but the man – if ever I were to wager a man were a magician I'd place my bets on him. Perhaps we can convince him to broker a deal with the new king and –"

"Enough with the magicians!" the town head roared, finally reaching the end of his patience. "We cannot hope for magic to save us! We need to ask the prince regent to provide for us, like he should."

"Ha!" Daven the woodcutter spat out. "Have fun with that, Fred! I'd like to see our new *king* provide for anyone but himself."

Fred winced. "Prince regent," he corrected. "And we have to at least ask. It is his duty to hear us out."

"And will you go to barter with him?"

He shook his head. "I fear he will not listen to me. His Royal Highness is young, and impulsive. I believe it better to send a more *attractive* messenger."

Everyone knew what he was getting at – he planned to send a woman. A young, pretty woman who might tempt Kilian Hale into helping them on a whim. A whim was all they needed, after all. And rumour had it that he was just as handsome as his father had been in his glory days. The problem was, of course, his horrible attitude. When it came right down to it the woman of Alder loved Gabriel, his older brother, and not Kilian, who was as likely to imprison a woman as he was to bed her.

And so it was that nobody in the hall seemed very enthusiastic about volunteering to be a messenger, something which Elina wholeheartedly agreed with.

*Clearly the town can't solve anything until someone has spoken to the prince regent,* she thought as she silently made her way to the door. *I'm not needed here. I'll just slip out and –*

"Send the magician's girl!"

Elina froze. She dared not turn, for she knew all eyes were on her.

"Yes, send Miss Brodeur!" Daven agreed enthusiastically. "She's certainly pretty enough, and her link to the magician can't hurt."

Of all the times for someone in Alder to admit that Elina was attractive to look at, she would not have picked this moment. She'd been used to everyone ignoring her – for men to barely spare her a glance because of her bastard status and foreign appearance. It was something which she had loathed before. It had made her feel unwanted and ugly.

To be told she was pretty enough to be used as bait for Kilian Hale was *not* what Elina had wanted to hear. But the general murmur of agreement filling her ears told her the town had already made up their mind. Reluctantly she turned, keeping her expression as blank as possible as she took in the faces of the people in the hall. Most of them were looking at her with their usual distaste, though there was a sick layer of satisfaction behind their eyes at the idea of sending their least favourite townsperson to do their dirty work that hadn't been there before.

Frederick raised an eyebrow at her. "Miss Brodeur, would you be willing to do this?"

Elina wanted so badly to say no. But what would that achieve? She and her mother would only further be ignored. They needed to maintain a steady stream of business if they were to afford the medicine required to stop her mother's sickness from growing worse.

And Elina was sick herself. Sick of being lonely and ignored. If she could somehow convince the prince regent to help the town then surely she would not be so hated. She might become liked. Respected, even. She'd settle for merely being acknowledged.

So she nodded. "I can leave now, if it pleases you," she said demurely, though inside she was fired up and ready to shout at them all to see what she was doing for people who did not care for her.

*See how selfless I'm being!* Elina wanted to scream. *See what I'm going to do for the ungrateful lot of you!*

She said neither of these things.

With a sigh of relief at how easy and painless choosing a messenger had turned out to be, Frederick smiled at her. Elina couldn't help but flinch - nobody ever smiled at her, least of all the town head. She ran off without another word, knowing that if she spoke she'd say something she'd regret.

*I can't disappoint them,* she thought as she made her

way towards the forest. *If I disappoint them I'll be in an even worse position than I was before. To improve my status I have to succeed.*

Elina stopped by a patch of ice and inspected her face. Her hair was braided and wrapped around her head, which was how she usually wore it. A few curly tendrils had broken loose; she used her fingers to shape them properly. In the permanent grey of winter her hair seemed dull and dark compared to the rest of the people of Alder, but Elina could do nothing about this.

She stared at her reflection for another few seconds, the green of her irises as bottomless as the pine trees she was about to pass under. She would never look like she belonged in Alder.

She'd have to earn her place there instead.

# Chapter Two

***Kilian***

It took Kilian precisely two minutes of consciousness to come to the conclusion that he didn't want to get out of bed. His head was killing him, he was freezing, and his shoulder ached from having slept on it badly. He glanced at the mostly-empty bottle of vodka lying on the floor and winced.

*That was definitely full when I started drinking yesterday.*

With a groan he threw himself back against his pillows. But just when Kilian decided that, as king, he could simply choose to remain in bed no matter what anybody said, he heard a knock on the door. He ignored it, of course, but it didn't go away.

"Who is it?!" he roared, immediately regretting having shouted when his head rang painfully in response.

"Your Royal Highness, the messenger from Alder is seeking an audience again," came the timid voice of a servant Kilian didn't care to recognise the voice of.

"Send her away," he replied, waving a dismissive hand at the door even though the servant couldn't see it.

"Ah, you see, Your Royal Highness," the man said hesitantly, "as regent you really are obligated to listen to the spokespeople of your country, and this is the fifth time you've turned her away –"

"I am aware of my obligations," Kilian bit back. He rubbed his head. "Fine then. Don't turn her away, but don't let her in, either. Let me see what she will do whilst blatantly being ignored."

He could tell the servant didn't like Kilian's response one bit, but he didn't care. Shivering as he forced himself out of bed, he threw on a long overcoat that lay abandoned on the floor, staring dolefully at the blackened, empty fireplace opposite his bed in the process. He was about to call out for his personal servant to see to getting a new fire started, but then Kilian remembered that he'd fired him.

He'd fired most of the castle staff, truth be told. He couldn't stand them. All hired by his father or his elder brother. All of them judging every disappointing move Kilian made as if they expected nothing more from him than self-indulgent depravity.

Well, if that's what they expected then that's what they'd get. Kilian had kept on barely enough staff to keep torches lit and food cooking in the kitchen. He enjoyed the solitude. If he could get away with it he'd have fired every last soul in the castle – including himself.

Kilian never wanted to be king, even in a temporary capacity, and he wanted it even less now that it had been forced upon him.

Staggering over to the tall window in his room, which overlooked the grounds to the front of the castle and allowed him to gaze across the forest to the town of Alder, Kilian felt his mood worsen. The weather was truly awful – the last time it had been this bad he'd been just three years old. That time, the winter had been despicable simply through bad luck. The current bout of bad weather had nothing to do with luck, bad or otherwise, just like the twenty years of *good* winters that preceded it.

Kilian didn't want to think about that.

Clutching his overcoat tighter around himself against the cold, he gazed down to the heavy iron front doors of the castle. A woman stood there, huddled into her cloak and looking thoroughly miserable. This was, indeed, the fifth time in as many days that the messenger from Alder had coming seeking an audience with him. He had to admire her tenacity.

*I suppose the town must be getting desperate,* he thought, looking up at the endless white sky and its blinding, heavy snow. *The weather has been awful ever since my father died, and it's my fault. Not that I care. If they die that's one less thing for me to pretend to worry about.*

All Kilian had to do was keep the throne warm for his brother's return. Gabriel had been at war since summer, fighting in the borders for some reason or other that Kilian had never deemed important enough to remember. Any day now he'd come back – triumphant or otherwise – and Kilian would be free of his responsibilities. He could leave the castle. Leave the country. He could go wherever he wanted.

In the meantime he was stuck inside a miserable, never-ending snowstorm. How could anyone expect him to *actually* do his job well when he'd never wanted it? His father should never have forced the position onto his youngest son if he'd wanted the kingdom taken care of.

But his father was dead and his brother gone. Now all Kilian could do was try to wrangle out some form of amusement to fill his days until he was free of the damn castle.

*And I guess she'll have to do,* he thought, a sly smile on his face as he gazed once more down at the woman in her blue cloak, almost invisible through the blizzard.

Kilian threw off his overcoat just long enough to dress in a white shirt and pair of trousers before sliding the coat back on top; his teeth were already chattering by the time he huddled against the fabric once more. His head was still killing him, so Kilian picked up the mostly-empty bottle of vodka from the floor and swallowed what was left. Fighting the immediate urge to vomit, he laced on a pair of boots, dragged a hand through his long, unkempt hair and slammed his door open.

Nobody was in the corridor, as expected. He wondered if he'd have to stop by the kitchen in order to get something for the pain in his head, though Kilian did not possess the patience to do so. When he reached the throne room he collapsed onto the overly-decorated chair, swinging his legs over one of the armrests as he dipped his head back over the other.

"Bring her in!" he called out to nobody in particular; he wasn't sure if anybody was even within earshot. "And get me some wine. In fact, bring me wine before you bring the girl." Kilian had priorities, after all, even if nobody else agreed with them. His first and foremost priority was always to be as drunk as he could physically get away with being, and he was at least a bottle of wine too sober for his own tastes.

A scrabbling by the door to the throne room told Kilian that his orders had been heard. Impatiently he waited for someone to bring his alcohol. When they did it was accompanied by bread, meats and cheeses. He waved that away.

"Did I say I needed food?" he demanded. But, upon feeling his stomach pinch in response, he waved the servant back. "Never mind. Keep it here. Now go away and fetch the girl."

Kilian scratched his chin as he guzzled down his first goblet of wine. A fine layer of stubble was growing; he needed to shave. He hadn't had cause to do so for days, though.

*When was the last time I had a woman?* he wondered. It had been at least two weeks. Resolving to have one sent to his rooms later that day, he shifted slightly on the throne when the sound of soft, light footsteps made their way towards him.

When the woman pulled down her snow-covered hood Kilian froze.

"Your R-Royal Highness," she said, shivering heavily as she struggled to bow. "M-my name is Elina Brodeur, and I c-come on behalf of Alder to seek your help."

But he wasn't listening. Kilian had never seen a woman like Elina Brodeur from his own country before. She stood out, dark and strange against the snow, reminding him of a man who had once come to the castle twenty years ago.

He straightened up on the throne and cleared his throat.

"You're the magician's girl."

# Chapter Three

***Elina***

The inside of Kilian Hale's castle was barely warmer than it had been outside. Elina's teeth were chattering so loudly in her skull that she barely heard the man's question. Well, it wasn't a question; more a statement of fact.

The prince regent looked at her with an expression of mild interest. "Well, aren't you?" he demanded.

Elina nodded. "He impregnated my mother, yes, but I would not say he was my father, and neither I his girl."

To her surprise Kilian snorted in amusement. "No, I guess not," he said. He settled back against the throne, pouring more wine down his throat before continuing. "So, Miss...?"

"Brodeur. Elina Brodeur. Daughter of Lily Brodeur –"

"Yes, yes, I don't care. You came here seeking my

help. What help exactly is it that you need?"

Something told Elina that Kilian knew exactly what the people of Alder needed. Going by his attitude, and the rate at which he was consuming wine, she concluded that he had merely approved an audience with her to provide himself with some kind of entertainment. The castle was empty, after all.

Disconcertingly so.

"Where is everyone?" Elina asked, glancing around the cavernous, dusty throne room. When she had imagined the inside of the castle this was not what she'd had in mind at all.

Kilian frowned. "Did I grant you an audience for you to criticise where I live?"

"I - no, I just -"

"Then tell me why you are here."

Elina struggled not to bristle against the man's standoffish attitude. He was royalty; he was *allowed* to be standoffish. She took in a somewhat shuddering breath, for she was still freezing. "This winter has hit Alder very hard. Too hard. We are running low on provisions - food, cloth, medicine, stone -"

"So you want me to provide the town with more?"

Elina kept her gaze steady. "Yes."

"Denied."

"...excuse me?"

"You heard me," Kilian said, glancing at Elina out of the corner of his eye with a smirk on his face that was begging for her to react. "No. I will not help your stupid town. You can all die. Now if that was all..."

"You can't be serious!"

"Oh, but I am."

"But so many people really *will* die if you cannot help - this isn't a joke!" Elina took a few steps forward, slipping on the snow that had fallen from her cloak and melted on the floor.

Kilian merely chuckled. "All the better for the kingdom if there are fewer people for me to rule. And besides," he pointed to one of the long, narrow windows, which were white with snow, "this kind of winter is made for culling the herd. You shouldn't expect everyone in Alder to survive this. So why even try to save them?"

Elina was torn between speaking her mind and keeping polite. This cruel man was her king, even if only until his far more capable brother returned. If she couldn't reason with him then the entire town would suffer.

She bowed her head. "Please, Your Royal Highness, I beg you to reconsider. I understand your sentiment, but -"

"You do, do you? And why would you understand such a deadly sentiment?"

"Because the people of Alder don't exactly like me, and I don't exactly like them, either."

Kilian seemed to consider this. "You would wish them dead for such a reason?"

"No," Elina murmured, shaking her head, "but I have thought it nonetheless. Thinking such a thing and allowing such a thing to happen are different, though."

"Not when you're king, they're not," he joked.

Elina looked up; Kilian was watching her carefully with eyes as pale as glass. They were not the brilliant blue of the people of Alder; instead, they were as icy grey as the snow outside the window. Elina found them unsettling.

She supposed Kilian really was handsome, though his long, pale blonde hair was tangled and knotted down his back. His sharp jawline was covered in stubble, and it looked as though he had hardly bothered to dress for meeting Elina. He wasn't wearing enough to combat the cold which, upon further notice, had resulted in the man shivering almost as much as Elina was in her snow-sodden clothes.

He frowned at her. "What are you looking at?"

"You aren't wearing enough. You'll catch a cold."

"Says the woman currently half frozen to death."

"I wouldn't be if I had been granted an audience earlier, *Your Royal Highness.*"

Elina didn't know why she was baiting Kilian, but if the man truly wasn't going to help Alder then she didn't see why she had to remain polite.

*He could lock me up in a cell and let me freeze to death, I suppose, but if that will be Alder's fate anyway then what does it matter?*

Kilian brought his glass up to his cruel mouth and drank deeply. He swept his eyes up and down Elina, which she forced herself not to shy away from.

"You say your town does not like you. Why is that?"

Surprised by the question, Elina carefully considered her answer before replying. "It isn't so much that they dislike me – that would involve them actually knowing me first. They simply do not wish to acknowledge my existence."

"Because of the magician?"

She nodded. "They don't like how different I look. And I was born out of wedlock, and my mother had many suitors at the time. She shamed my grandparents by doing so, though they loved her too much to let her - or me - go. Fortunately my mother is a talented seamstress, so she took over my grandfather's tailor shop, so the town's scorn for me means little and less."

"And yet, clearly, that's a lie."

Elina said nothing. Of course it was a lie.

"You would not be here if you didn't care for them," Kilian continued, almost to himself. "So tell me, Elina Brodeur, how *much* do you care for this town that hates you? What would you do for them?"

"I...what are you asking of me, Your Royal Highness?"

His lips twisted into a smile; Elina did not like the look of it at all.

"Become my personal servant. Wait on me, tend to my fires and my room and serve me food and wine. Do my bidding, no matter how humiliating that may be. Do all this and I shall provide Alder with the provisions it needs."

"Surely you must have far more qualified servants for such a role?" Elina asked, dumbfounded by the request.

Kilian shrugged. "No. I fired them all."

"You - why?"

"You may have told me about your pathetic, sob story excuse for a life, tailor girl, but that does not mean

I have to tell you mine."

Elina said nothing. Kilian clearly wanted her to lose her temper. Or maybe he didn't; maybe he simply always spoke like this. Either way, Elina hated him for it. Frederick had wanted a young woman to beg Kilian for help on the hope that he'd take a liking to her and help her on a whim.

*Well, this is clearly a* whim, *but not the kind the town was thinking of.* Elina supposed this way was better. She hadn't wanted Kilian to take a *liking* to her in the way they'd been hoping. She didn't want to end up in his bed, giving up her virginity for the sake of a town who responded to her mother losing hers with disgust.

"...is there a limit to what you would have me do, as your servant?" she asked quietly, keeping her eyes downcast.

Kilian finished his wine and threw the glass to the floor, where it smashed. He picked up a thick slice of bread and tore off the crust, gnawing on it as he considered Elina's question.

"Maybe. Maybe not. I guess that's something you'll find out after accepting it."

"You act as if I *will* accept."

"Do you really have a choice? Something tells me you don't."

Elina hated being told this. Because of course she didn't really have a choice; if the town died then so would her mother. At least, for her, Elina had to endure the whims of Kilian Hale.

"I will not live in the castle," she said, looking up at Kilian as she spoke. He didn't seem to like this at all.

"You will. What if I require your assistance at night?"

"My mother is poorly; I will not leave her."

"Then have her live here too."

"We have the shop. It's our livelihood. I will not move her, or me. This is the only way I'll accept your proposal."

*This is the only way I can* tolerate *your proposal.*

Finally, after what seemed like minutes but was actually seconds, Kilian swallowed the bread he was chewing and nodded.

"Fine; live in the town that hates you. But you have to arrive at the castle before sunrise and stay until after my evening meal."

"Which is...?"

He grinned. "As late as I can make it."

Elina felt her temple twitch in irritation. "How long must I act as your servant?"

"As long as I want." And then, at the look of indignation on Elina's face, clarified, "Until winter ends. You will serve me for as long as your town needs assistance."

"And you will provide assistance immediately?"

"Yes."

Something told Elina her idea of immediately and Kilian's idea of immediately were entirely different things. But she didn't want to push her drunk, cruel king too far, in case he changed his mind.

With a yawn, Kilian stretched his arms above his head until his spine cracked in several places. He looked at Elina from heavy-lidded eyes hazy with alcohol.

"First order of business, Elina: run me a bath."

Elina had never wanted to do anything less in all her life.

# Chapter Four

***Kilian***

"Where are the baths situated?"

"Oh, I have one in my room. Follow me."

Kilian lazily unfolded himself from his throne, sweeping past Elina as he exited through the door, not stopping to check if she was following him.

"Clean up in there," he ordered the same man who had served him food and wine. "Some utter heathen smashed my wine glass on the floor."

When Elina rushed to match Kilian's strides he did not slow down to accommodate her. It was far more amusing to watch the frozen, soaking woman struggle to keep up with him.

"I'm assuming you know how to light fires and prepare bathwater," he said.

"Of course I do."

He opened the door to his chambers and gestured towards the large, ornate bathtub. "Then get to it."

Elina stared at it in confusion. Her gaze lowered to the floor beneath it, which was scratched and damaged as if someone had literally dragged the heavy, ceramic tub into the room.

She glanced at Kilian. "Something tells me this wasn't supposed to be in here."

"It's easier to roll out of the bath and straight into bed if it's here," he explained simply, leaving Elina's side to wander about his room in search of a forgotten bottle of wine or vodka. Finding none, he collapsed on top of his bed. "If you don't get a fire going soon you're liable to genuinely freeze to death, so I suggest you be quick about it."

Elina straightened up at the comment. She unclasped her cloak and hung it from the door without waiting for permission to do so; in its absence Kilian could properly see her figure in the well-fitted, dark blue dress she wore.

*Not bad at all,* he thought appreciatively. *Not as tall as the rest of the women in Alder. Curvier, too.*

Kilian contented himself with watching Elina scurry around his room, cleaning the hearth before throwing fresh logs into the fireplace.

"There's more wood in the room over there," Kilian drawled, half-heartedly pointing to an adjoining storage room. "There's a water reserve and bowls for filling the tub in there, too."

Elina remained impassive as she said, "Why would the prince regent have a storage room for such things attached to his private chambers?"

"Because said prince regent is always cold, and likes to have firewood close at hand."

"So why don't you have a fire going constantly, if you're always cold?"

"Because I fired the staff, or have you forgotten?"

Elina paused. "You don't know how to light your own fire?"

"Why should I have to know how to do that?"

"Well if you're going to fire your staff it would be useful to know."

Kilian smiled. "Hence why *you're* here."

Sighing, and wearing an expression that very much suggested she thought Kilian was useless, Elina got to work starting a fire. Before long she had lit a spark, then the twists of paper she'd carefully placed between the logs caught fire, then eventually the wood itself. Within minutes a proper fire was merrily burning, though it was yet to give off any proper heat.

Wordlessly Elina moved through to the storage room to fill up a large bowl with water. When she gasped and returned with dripping wet, steaming hands, Kilian smirked.

"Have you never felt hot water before?" he asked sardonically.

"You have a thermal pool beneath the castle."

"Indeed I do. There are hot springs to the back of the castle, in fact."

Elina stared at her hands as if she couldn't believe it. "Why not use the hot springs to bathe, then?"

He couldn't be bothered answering such a complicated question. Instead, Kilian pointed to the window. "Have you forgotten about the blizzard? Why would I wish to bathe in *that*?"

She wrinkled her nose. "I guess not. At least this will make filling your bath much easier."

"Lucky for you."

Elina said nothing, though she removed the top layer of her dress and rolled up the sleeves of her undershirt before continuing to fill a large bowl with water, emptying it into the bathtub before refilling it once more and repeating the action over and over again until the tub was full.

The fire was well and truly hot by then; Kilian sighed in relief when he was finally able to feel his toes. In the flickering light he could see that Elina's hair was not quite as dark as her magician father, whose appearance was burned onto his brain even though he tried to forget about the man. It was almost burnished – a deep, intense copper colour that Kilian had never seen before. He thought it matched Elina's golden skin perfectly. Though she was still sodden, and her braid was a mess around her head, Kilian concluded that she really was quite lovely to look at.

*I've picked a good servant,* he thought, eagerly stripping off his boots and clothes in order to throw himself into the scalding bath. He wasn't expecting Elina to cry out in surprise and turn away in horror.

"Your – Your Royal Highness! You might have given me some warning!"

Kilian laughed as he eased himself into the water, which turned into a low moan of satisfaction as the heat seeped into his muscles. He leaned his head back to look at Elina. "What's wrong, Elina?" he asked casually. "Have you never seen a naked man before? Or is it simply that you've never seen a naked *prince* before?"

"I – you clearly know the answer to your question, Your Royal Highness," she stammered, keeping her back firmly to Kilian. "You don't even have anything to put in the bathwater! It's completely clear."

He shrugged. "Why would I bother putting anything in the water? All I need it for is taking away the cold."

Elina risked a glance over her shoulder; Kilian was satisfied to see her face was flushed. "You cannot clean yourself properly with water only, Your Royal –"

"You can stop it with the *Your Royal Highness* thing, Elina. Come over here."

She shook her head.

"Come here. That's an order."

Desperately looking like she wanted to protest, Elina crept towards the bathtub until she stood behind Kilian's head. He arched his neck further to stare at her as she looked down at him. This close up, he could see that Elina did not quite share the same eye colour as her father – not as far as Kilian could remember. Her eyes were greener, and the colour seemed purer, though in the firelight it still contained a few flecks of gold which he clearly remembered the magician's eyes having, too.

Elina darted her eyes away uncertainly. "What is it?"

"Comb my hair."

She looked as if she might object but, upon weighing up whether there would be much point, she drooped her shoulders and nodded. "Where's your comb?"

"By the mirror."

And so Elina retrieved the comb and, with obvious reluctance, slid Kilian's hair out from beneath his head to hang over the edge of the tub.

"There's a chair over there that you can sit on," he said, indicating over to his left. So Elina retrieved that, too, and sat down by Kilian's head. She seemed to hesitate before touching his hair, but when she did he said, "And be gentle, of course. No hurting me just because you can."

A flash of irritation crossed her face as if she was insulted that Kilian might suggest she would do such a thing. He remained on edge until Elina ran the comb through his hair a few times, stopping when she came upon knots and tangles to carefully unravel them with deft fingers. When it became apparent that she was going to do her job properly, he relaxed.

"You're very good at this," he murmured after a few minutes.

"I've worked out worse tangles in the wool and thread we use in the shop," Elina replied, voice quiet.

And then there was only the crackle of the fire to break the silence, though Kilian did not feel the need to add to the noise. Usually the whip of the wind outside was all he could hear but, for the first time in months, the wind was calm. Kilian was warm, relaxed, and actually enjoying himself - he couldn't remember the last time all three of those things had occurred at the same time. He wondered if he would have also enjoyed himself if he wasn't drunk, though he didn't care enough to find out.

When Elina finally stopped combing his hair he opened his eyes, which Kilian had not been aware were closed in the first place. He almost said thank you.

Almost.

"Where do you keep your clothes?" Elina asked as she put the chair and comb back where she had found them.

He gestured to a room adjacent to the dressing table. "In there."

Elina disappeared inside. For a few minutes all Kilian heard were the sounds of her rummaging through his things; he wondered what she was doing. When she returned carrying a fine, woollen shirt and long, soft leggings before laying them on the bed he frowned.

"What are those for?"

"Wear them to bed. They'll keep you warm."

He stared at the clothes incredulously. "They're so thin. I don't believe you."

She put her hands on her hips. "You have nothing to lose by listening to me."

"I guess not," he replied, sinking beneath the water until it only just reached his hairline. When he resurfaced Elina looked away quickly. He grinned slyly. "How can you be so embarrassed by a naked body? How old are you?"

"...twenty."

"Ah, of course. That makes sense, what with the magician and all. So you're a twenty-year-old woman - two years past marrying age - and you're still this innocent?"

She bristled. "I shouldn't have to explain myself to the likes of you."

"The likes of me?" Kilian parroted back in interest. "Tell me, Elina, what do you mean by that?"

"I - you know what I mean, clearly. Otherwise you

wouldn't keep looking at me the way you do, like I'm an object."

*Huh. She's sharper than I thought.*

"I guess that's true. In which case I apologise."

"That doesn't sound sincere at all."

He quirked an eyebrow. "So you won't accept even a semblance of an apology from me, despite the fact I'm the ruler of this land?"

Elina winced as she slid back into the outer layer of her dress and retrieved her cloak, which was stiff and dark with water. "You're the one who doesn't want me to call you *Your Royal Highness.* Something tells me the last thing you want is for me to treat you like a king or regent or anything remotely similar."

And then she opened the door and left without another word, though Kilian had not given her leave to go. Indeed, it was barely mid-afternoon. Yet he allowed it, for it was the boldest move anyone had made against him in a long, long time.

Hours later, when Kilian retired to bed, he decided to humour Elina's whims and dress in the clothes she had picked out. They felt thin and insubstantial; he prepared himself for a long, sleepless, freezing night beneath the covers.

Instead he fell asleep within minutes, as warm as if he were still in the bath, Elina combing his hair.

# Chapter Five

***Elina***

"The prince finally granted you an audience?!"

"That's certainly one way to put it," Elina grimaced as she shed off every layer of her sodden clothing and slid into the bath her mother had prepared. She thought of Kilian's on-demand hot water supply with envy.

Lily Brodeur stared at her daughter, eyes bright with interest. "What do you mean by that? How did it go?"

"I...mama, how could that man be our king?"

Her mother laughed lightly. "So he really is still that bad-tempered. I always hoped he'd grow out of it. At least he won't be ruling for long."

"You talk as if you know him."

"I made clothes for Kilian and Gabriel once, back before I knew I was pregnant with you," she smiled. "Well, I helped my father make them. I went with him to the castle to deliver them. Gabriel was every inch the young prince - so elegant and composed - and he was only eight! But little Kilian was not quite four, and I had never met a child so tempestuous. He threw the clothes I made him in the fire!"

Elina gawked at her mother. "That can't possibly be a true story."

"Oh, but it is, I assure you. I wonder if he remembers?"

"He didn't seem to recognise my surname," Elina said, "though he was drunk, so that might explain it."

Lily looked at her in concern. "So what happened? You tried so hard to speak with him – I somehow doubt *my* daughter would leave without succeeding at what she sought out to do."

The comment warmed Elina's heart for a moment, though it was instantly doused as she explained her deal with the cruel, obnoxious sham of a ruler that was Kilian Hale. She watched as shock, disbelief and concern darkened her mother's pale face, grimly certain that she would try to talk her daughter out of her deal with the proverbial devil.

"Elina, you can't possibly –"

"It's only until winter passes," Elina spoke over her mother quickly. "Alder needs the supplies, mama. And *we* need Alder. We'll die along with everyone else if we don't get the help we need to get through the next few months."

Lily looked away from her daughter, discomfited. "I don't like it, Elina. If Kilian truly is as unreasonable as he seems then he might well simply be taking advantage of you with no intention of helping us at all."

"I have to at least try, mama. If, after two weeks, he still hasn't sent any provisions, I'll tell him the deal is off."

"He doesn't sound like the kind of man who would let you do that."

Elina sighed as she got out of the bathtub and towelled herself dry. "What would you have me do?"

"We could leave."

Lily's voice was very quiet as she stared at the fire currently roaring in the hearth. Elina shrugged on a shirt and some trousers and sat by her mother, inspecting her face. Her pallor was sickly and almost green, and her hands shook slightly. She was growing weaker by the day. A knot tightened in Elina's stomach at the unimaginable thought that her mother would not last the winter.

"Maybe when winter passes and your health returns," Elina said, forcing a smile onto her face. She unravelled the braid from around her head - her hair was still wet from the snow - and combed it through until she'd worked through the tangles in her wavy hair.

She was starkly reminded of combing Kilian's hair mere hours ago, though she didn't want to think about him. Once Elina had unpicked the knots, Kilian's hair had been lustrous, soft and shiny. It was paler than the blonde hair of the people of Alder, just as his eyes were paler, too. It was almost as if he were made of ice himself.

*That would explain his callous attitude,* Elina thought as she rebraided her hair, letting it hang down her back like a rope as she laced on a pair of dry boots and a dark green cloak that had belonged to her grandfather.

"Where are you going, Elina?" her mother sputtered in surprise. She coughed several times into her hands, taking a few ragged breaths before continuing. "You only just got back. And your hair is still wet."

She glanced out of the window. "I want to stop by the apothecary whilst the weather is still calm. I won't be long, don't worry."

As she had done with Kilian, Elina left without another word. Outside the snow was still falling, but it was soft and gentle and almost pleasant. It had been like that since Elina had combed Kilian's hair in the bath, flying through the air almost silently outside his window.

*Don't think about him in that bath.* Elina's face grew warm despite the cold, and she shook her head to clear it of her thoughts. She struggled along the ice-encrusted road until, with some relief, she reached the apothecary.

It was closed.

"Of course," she said aloud, watching her breath form a tiny cloud in front of her face. She couldn't go home without buying more medicine for her mother – their stocks were too low, and the way her mother was now Elina highly doubted she would get much sleep.

*Maybe Erik or his wife are in the tavern,* she thought, heading towards the establishment despite the fact she hated the place. Elina had never been welcome there; even when she had visited with her mother and grandparents as a child she had been shunned. It was the worst place to be ignored, surrounded by people having a good time. Enjoying themselves. Living in a world in which they pretended Elina did not exist.

And yet she pushed through the door of Gill's tavern despite all of that, because her mother's health was more important than her pride. Everybody looked at her as she walked across the bar, looking for Erik, the apothecary. Nobody asked her about how she was faring trying to broker a deal with Kilian.

She could tell by their faces they all hoped she would fail, even though their livelihoods depended on her succeeding.

*They can go to hell,* Elina thought as she concluded that neither Erik nor his wife were in the tavern. But then she caught sight of something unusual: black hair. Long, lustrous, wavy black hair. When the head of the woman whose hair it belonged to turned Elina saw one of the most beautiful people she had ever set eyes upon.

When she smiled at her, Elina looked down at the floor. "You stand out almost as much as me and Adrian," the woman said. Her voice was low and musical; lilting. "Won't you sit with us?"

"I - can I?"

She laughed softly. "Of course! You seem just about as welcome as us in here. Won't you tell us your name?" She indicated to the man standing behind her, who was looking for an available table. He flashed Elina a grin that she could only describe as *wolfish.* He had the strangest eyes she had ever seen - amber, like a sunset.

"Elina. I'm Elina Brodeur," Elina found herself saying, still enraptured by the two incredibly attractive people in front of her.

"I'm Scarlett Duke," the woman said, "and this idiot is Adrian Wolfe. Adrian, can't you find a table?"

The man named Adrian shook his handsome head. "There are none to be found. I guess we're eating up in our room. Miss Brodeur, who were you looking for when you entered the tavern?"

She was surprised by the man's observation; had the strangers been watching her since she entered the place?

"Um...the apothecary," she said. "My mother is sick."

A flash of concern crossed Scarlett's face. "What ails her?"

"It's her lungs, for the most part. But she's always been frail. The cold has affected her badly this winter."

Scarlett glanced at Adrian. "How much stock do we have left?"

"Enough," he said. "Miss Brodeur, if you don't mind accompanying us up to our room I think we can help you."

Elina followed them numbly without really thinking. She wasn't used to people talking to her outside of the shop, and even then all conversation was kept short and professional. The only other stranger who'd talked to her this much was Kilian Hale, and he didn't count, because Elina wished he didn't exist.

When they reached the room Scarlett rummaged through a large trunk of vials, bottles and boxes that Elina would never have been able to make heads nor tails of.

"Let's see..." Scarlett murmured. "We have some eucalyptus oil from Asia - that'll help with your mother's breathing - and, let's see...peppermint, thyme and ginger for coughing and fever, and...oh! Powdered willow bark, for pain relief." She dumped several items in Elina's arms without warning. "Brew the herbs as a tea and sweeten it with honey. Don't let her take more than one finger joint's worth of willow bark in a given five hour period. You can put some eucalyptus oil in your mother's bathwater or add it to some boiling water and have her breathe in the steam. You can also pour a few drops on her pillow, to ease her sleep."

Elina stared at her in disbelief. "How do you know all of this?"

Scarlett grinned; she tilted her head in Adrian's direction, who was drinking a tankard of ale he'd brought up from downstairs. "He taught me most everything I know, believe it or not."

Considering Elina had heard rumours that Adrian Wolfe was a magician at the town hall meeting, she did not doubt it. He really *did* look like a magician... whatever that meant. It was probably his eyes, or the white streak in his dark hair.

He scoffed at Scarlett's answer. "Believe it or not, indeed. I am very well educated."

"No need to show off, Adrian."

Elina's eyes darted between the two of them. "H-how much do I owe you for all of this?" she asked, lifting up her armful of remedies.

"Oh, just take it for free," Scarlett said. "Only... promise that you'll keep us company whilst we're in Alder. We could do with talking to someone local who'll be honest with us."

"...about what?"

"That depends," Adrian said. "How honest will you be?"

"Certainly more honest than the people downstairs would be."

He laughed amiably. "Oh, I like you. So tell me, Miss Brodeur; why can I smell magic upon you?"

She froze. Magic? On *her?*

"Adrian, don't scare her," Scarlett chided. She touched Elina's arm gently. "Pay him no mind. Adrian is a little more...sensitive to some things than most folk are."

"Are you here because of magic?" Elina asked.

"Possibly," Scarlett replied, her answer decidedly ambiguous. "We don't know yet. But now we're stuck here either way. So might you keep us company some nights and help us work out what's going on?"

Elina knew she should say no. She had too much going on with her mother's sickness and her stupid deal with Kilian Hale. But how could she resist the allure of *magic?* Elina was deathly curious.

Then she spotted a bag of bath salts inside Scarlett's trunk. Thinking of Kilian's bath, and how she never wanted to see him naked again if she could avoid it, she smiled slightly.

"Give me those bath salts and I'll gladly help you however I can."

# CHAPTER SIX

***Kilian***

Elina Brodeur was acting unnecessarily servile. Kilian wanted her to snap and talk back to him, like she had done when she'd first left the castle. But she hadn't; instead, she demurely obeyed all of Kilian's orders without so much as a word of complaint. It infuriated him to no end.

And so Kilian got drunk, as he always did. He got so royally drunk he'd put the local alcoholics of Alder to shame. Not that he could know this for a fact, given he couldn't leave the castle, but the sentiment was there.

"Elina, get over here," he drawled. Kilian was spread lazily over his bed, the sheets crumpled and creased beneath him as he rolled around with a bottle of vodka. He was well and truly wasted; so wasted, in fact, that he wasn't even aware that it was barely noon.

"Your Royal Highness, you have guests waiting for you in the throne room!" Elina exclaimed in horror when she dutifully rushed into Kilian's chambers.

"I told you not to call me that," he slurred.

"And yet I shall, because I have to," she replied, green eyes set with determination as she watched over the sprawling figure of the man who ruled her country, drunk out of his mind.

"But I am regent, and I told you not to. Dare you defy me?"

"Even so..."

Kilian knew she was being careful, and why; the fate of her entire town rested on her shoulders. He found it highly amusing that, in turn, what happened to Alder rested in *his* palms and that, if he failed to do anything to help them, it would be Elina who suffered for it. Elina, who hated the town that ignored her. Elina, who was trying to help them anyway.

He was determined to find out exactly *why* she was doing this.

*It can't only be because of her mother,* he opined. *She said her mother was sick, but so what? People get sick all the time. And it's not like I didn't offer to let them* both *stay in the castle. If her mother's health was all that mattered then Elina would have taken me up on that.*

"You really have to be in the throne room," Elina murmured, looking away when Kilian slid his hands beneath the waistband of his leggings to pull out the hem of his shirt. "Your guests have been waiting for a while, and I highly doubt they'll be as patient as I was when I sought an audience with you."

Kilian barked out a laugh. "Probably not. And yet I won't see them, but I saw you."

"Your Royal Highness –"

"Stop calling me that."

"But you *are* a prince, and regent, whether you want to be or not!"

Kilian sat up and grabbed Elina's sleeve, dragging her towards him. "And what would you say if I told you I *don't* want to be in this position?" he asked, eyes glittering dangerously. Fear flitted across her face for but half a second as she gulped, and then it was gone.

"I'd say that you not wanting to be king is hardly a revelation. That much is obvious."

"You dare say that to my face but refuse to do away with my title? You make no sense, Elina."

She pulled her sleeve out of Kilian's grasp. "Maybe not, but I do not have to explain myself to you, either way."

"Yes you do. I'm your king."

"...then act like one."

Elina uttered those words so quietly that Kilian, in his drunken haze, barely heard them. For some reason they stung, though he knew they were true. Outside the wind rattled the stone of the castle, threatening to break through the window. He considered for one wild moment to allow the weather to get even worse, simply to strand Elina here, with him.

*Let me watch her worry over her stupid town and her stupid mother who thought herself talented enough to make me clothes, whilst I lie here getting so drunk she does not know what to do with me.*

For of course Kilian knew who Elina's mother was. Or, at least, he had finally remembered after sobering up the day after they'd made their deal. Though he'd been very young Kilian remembered the encounter acutely. That winter had been bitterly cold, after all; his mother wanted him and his brother Gabriel wrapped in the warmest fabrics. Kilian had not wanted clothes spun by simple-minded commoners, though in truth the clothes were finely made. He'd thrown them in the fire, much to the horror of his parents.

If he were sober Kilian might have exhibited an ounce of shame remembering such an act. It hadn't simply been unbecoming of him, even at three – it had been unfair. The clothes had been lovely. Going by Elina's dresses and cloaks, her mother had only grown more talented in her skill with a needle. Lily Brodeur and her father had merely sought to clothe him in fabrics warm enough to keep out the winter chill, as had Elina when she looked out the right clothes for Kilian to sleep in.

But even so, Kilian didn't care. They were only clothes, and the Brodeurs were mere commoners. They could do whatever they wanted – travel wherever they wanted – and yet they clung to the side of the stupid mountainside even as it threatened to kill them. It was beyond stupid.

And so he ignored Elina's comment to act more like a king because, at least for him, he had never been given a choice. Kilian had to be king even if he was terrible at it, so terrible he would be. Elina could literally choose to leave at any point.

But she didn't.

"See to my guests for me," he muttered, pulling a cover over his head as he took a swig from his bottle of vodka like a hungry newborn babe with milk.

"I cannot do that!" Elina protested. "I will not!"

"You would disobey a direct order from me?"

There was a pause. "If this is how you mean to treat me then yes. This was a mistake. You can keep your stupid deal; I won't be back again."

Kilian fell out of bed before he could stop himself.

"No!" he exclaimed, much louder than he had expected to speak. Elina's face went blank though he could tell she was, in truth, surprised. "No," Kilian repeated, calmer this time. He sat back down on his bed. "You're right; how could you possibly know how to deal with foreign diplomats? Go home. But come back tomorrow. I'll deal with them myself."

It was a back-handed apology if it could be called an apology at all. But it seemed to work for Elina, though Kilian doubted the same tactic would have the same effect a second time.

"Fine," she said, not looking him in the eye. "I shall take my leave, then."

She didn't say goodbye. She didn't even look at him. When Elina exited Kilian's bedroom he was tempted once more to trap her in the castle; to cause the snow to pile up so high and the wind to bite so harshly that she couldn't possibly take a single foot outside.

He resisted.

Instead, Kilian forced himself out of bed and into slightly more regal clothes, smoothed back his hair and left for the throne room.

*I hate diplomats,* he thought, sincerely wishing he was back in his room drinking himself unconscious.

# Chapter Seven

***Elina***

Elina hated Kilian's castle. It was cold and dark and empty and...lonely.

Very, very lonely.

She had thought her life in Alder was isolated; it was nothing compared to what the king's life must be like living in such cavernous halls all alone.

"He did that to himself," Elina muttered as she ran Kilian a bath. She'd been working for the man for close to a week now. He was yet to send any supplies or provisions to Alder, so the town was still dutifully ignoring Elina. For all they knew she had completely failed at her task and was simply hiding every day to avoid their scorn and judgement.

She hated it. Kilian had her work every menial task he could think of – which largely involved making fires, fetching him more alcohol and, on occasion, preparing and bringing him food. Most of the time he simply wanted to keep her near to insult people or complain to her about nothing in particular. Elina largely suspected that all he wanted was to hear the sound of his own voice – that it ultimately didn't matter who he was speaking to.

It still shocked her somewhat that Kilian had actually spoken to the diplomats who had sought an audience with him a few days prior. One of the remaining servants had informed Elina of this fact the following day, though what she was supposed to do with this information she had no clue. She knew the diplomats were from the country waging war against them – the people Kilian's older brother, Gabriel, was fighting.

*What can I do about that?* she wondered as she added the final bowl of water to the bath. *What did that servant hope to achieve from me knowing that Kilian* actually *did his job? Were they suggesting that it was now my job to ensure he always did his?*

That was something Elina didn't want to be in charge of at all, especially considering how much else she was currently responsible for. Still, with the remedies Scarlett and Adrian had given her at least she didn't have to worry so much about her mother's health; she finally seemed able to sleep and the feverish chills that had plagued her for weeks had abated. For that Elina was eternally grateful, and was determined to sit down with the mysterious pair to tell them everything they needed to know about Alder and its people.

*You smell of magic.*

Elina couldn't get Adrian Wolfe's words out of her head. She was dying to know what they meant – and how Adrian had sensed magic from her in the first place. She could only conclude that he really *was* a magician. It was exciting, given that Elina had never met a magician before despite her 'father' being one.

But the thought was driven out of her head for her when Kilian entered his chambers, drunk as usual. Elina suppressed a heavy eye roll when the man tumbled onto the bed with an exhausted sigh, as if his day had been long and hard instead of short and full of nothing.

It was then that Elina remembered the bath salts she had so foolishly asked Scarlett for, so she retrieved them from the bag she'd brought with her and dumped a load of them unceremoniously into the bathtub. They clouded the water immediately, foaming around the edges of the tub whilst emitting a pleasantly foreign, spicy scent; Elina relished the smell as she breathed it in.

Kilian coughed. "What have you put in my bath, woman?" he demanded as he stumbled over to investigate, eyes bleary, red and slightly unfocused.

"Bath salts," she explained. "They're good for your skin."

"They make the water look filthy," he replied, surveying the steaming bath with distaste.

"Why would I make my life that much harder by trying to coax you into a dirty bath? I'd only have to run you a new one afterwards if that were the case."

Kilian didn't seem to like Elina's infallible logic, but his near-constant desire to be warmer than he currently was overrode that dislike. With another grimace at the bath he pulled his shirt up and over his head before removing his boots and leggings, not bothering to turn from Elina as he undressed. She knew he did this because it embarrassed her, which only made her hatred for Kilian grow.

He did not respect her, not even in her capacity as a servant. She doubted he respected anyone at all.

But she *could* do something about Kilian's nakedness, at least whilst he was in the bath - namely covering him up with cloudy, steaming, exotically spiced water. And he didn't seem to have worked out her ulterior motives yet, which Elina was relieved about. She was fairly certain that if Kilian were aware of her intentions he would parade about naked in front of her just to make a point, no matter how cold he might be.

When he slid beneath the murky water's surface she bit back a noise of relief. It set Elina on edge to have the prince regent of her country stand in front of her in all his naked vulnerability, no matter how useless a ruler he was. She didn't want the implied responsibility of protecting him, after all. If someone were to come into Kilian's chambers looking to harm him, would he expect Elina to stand between him and his foe? She hoped not...for she certainly wouldn't do it.

"Comb my hair again, Elina," Kilian sighed, clearly already very content in his bath. So she retrieved his comb and the chair she'd sat on before and moved over to the bath and, without thinking, dunked the man's head beneath the water. She realised too late that she absolutely shouldn't have.

When Kilian broke the water's surface he was sputtering in indignation. "What on earth was that for?!"

Elina knew if she showed any weakness then he would take advantage of it. "You need to wash your hair," she explained simply. "And now it'll smell nice when it dries."

"Who cares if it smells nice?" Kilian muttered, though he settled into the bath once more and arched his neck back for Elina to comb his now soaking hair nonetheless.

As compensation for dunking his head underwater - which, now that she'd gotten away it, Elina could admit to having enjoyed immensely - she was particularly gentle with combing Kilian's hair. She worked through it with her fingers as much as the teeth of the ivory comb, rubbing her fingertips against his scalp to ensure no undissolved bath salts remained.

When Kilian emitted a low groan from the back of his throat, she paused. He flashed her a drunken, warning glare.

"Don't stop that," he ordered. "I like it. Keep going."

Elina put down the comb and gingerly placed her fingertips back on Kilian's scalp. She didn't *want* to massage his head. She didn't want to do anything that would make him happy, even though making him happy would undoubtedly help Alder. But that didn't stop her hating the man...and she knew she was good at head massages. Her grandmother taught her, whom people used to pay to have massage their heads and shoulders.

She knew she had to swallow her pride. Being contrary for the sake of it would get her nowhere except out in the cold with no food to survive the winter. So Elina got to work, slowly and softly moving her fingertips in small circles whilst gradually increasing their pressure against Kilian's scalp. He closed his eyes, leaning his head back just a little more as if urging Elina's fingers to come closer.

Outside the window all was still, which unsettled Elina. Not being able to hear the wind rattle the window frame or hailstones pounding the glass made her think that the eye of a storm must surely have hit, and that things were only going to get worse on her miserable walk back home.

Without thinking her fingers moved to Kilian's ears, sliding along their edge and down to his earlobes, which she rubbed between her fingertips before moving further down Kilian's neck and –

She stopped. Hands frozen in place on either side of Kilian's head, Elina wondered what had possessed her to travel further along his body than his ears. When Kilian opened his eyes and looked up at her they were hazy – no doubt from the alcohol, but Elina thought it might mean something else.

"I didn't tell you to stop, Elina," he murmured. Elina watched his lips as he spoke, which were wet from the bath. Her face grew red, though the heat from the fire did a good job of explaining that away. "Keep doing whatever you were doing."

With a small frown of uncertainty she crept her hands back up his head; Kilian responded by reaching up and covering her hands with his own, much larger ones. He pulled them down to his neck without saying a word.

Kilian didn't close his eyes this time. He kept them locked on Elina's face as she reluctantly worked out an inordinate amount of tension from his neck, moving onto his shoulders when he finally took his hands away from hers. But when she saw where his hands were going, even though the murky water obscured her from actually seeing anything, she recoiled away.

"I'm not – I'm not touching you for you to – to touch yourself!" she bit out, mortified.

Kilian's eyes flashed. "And why not? I'm the king. I can order you to do what I like."

Elina considered her next words very carefully. She took a deep breath. "Please do not ask me to do such a thing. I don't want to be part of your...bedroom activities."

He chuckled at the remark, though there was a hardness to his expression that indicated he did not much like this turn of events. "Very well," he said, still smiling, "you may go for the evening, since I clearly have some *bedroom activities* to attend to."

Elina could do nothing but stare at him, until Kilian's genial expression broke and he indicated towards the door with his head.

"Get out. You need not come to the castle tomorrow."

When Elina stepped outside the wind had picked back up again with a renewed ferocity; her face was pelted with hailstones which very quickly robbed her of the heat in her cheeks.

She had walked out of one kind of storm and into a new one. She didn't know which one was worse.

# Chapter Eight

***Kilian***

"Get out, get out," Kilian repeated, over and over again to his empty bedroom for nobody to hear but himself. He didn't understand: why had he reacted so physically to a *head massage?* Elina certainly hadn't intended it to be erotic in nature. He should know - he'd hired many a girl to perform exactly that kind of massage...only, they didn't stop at his shoulders.

It occurred to Kilian that he hadn't arranged for a woman to be brought to him since the day he'd decided Elina should be his servant. Clearly the tailor girl had unnecessarily distracted him. But he now had an insatiable thirst that needed quenched, so he barked out for a servant until one arrived.

They stared at him nervously; he didn't often let anyone into his chambers when he was bathing. "Bring a woman to the castle," he said. "Any young, pretty one will do." For a moment he thought about requesting she have brown hair, green eyes and sun-kissed skin, only to remember that likely the only girl in his entire country that fit that description was Elina.

The servant's eyes darted to the window. "Your Royal Highness, in such weather it might be –"

"Are you suggesting you cannot fulfil my orders?"

"Absolutely not! I – I shall see to it right away, sire."

The servant quickly retreated, leaving Kilian to his bath and his taut, frustrated body. Even *he* had to admit that he was getting too hot in the scalding water, though perhaps it was the scent of the bath salts that was getting to him and making him feel drowsy. Kilian wasn't sure what the steam smelled of exactly, other than the fact it was clearly exotic.

*I wonder if Elina knows what the scent is,* he thought as he hauled himself out of the bath, choosing to sit in front of the roaring fire to dry off instead of using a towel. An open bottle of wine that quite possibly had spoiled sat by the hearth; Kilian grabbed it and began eagerly swallowing the red liquid inside.

By the time a woman finally arrived at his door he had moved onto another bottle of wine, though Kilian had already been drunk before starting the first one. Now he was truly wasted.

The woman was young and pretty enough – all buttery hair, blue eyes and lithe limbs – but for some reason Kilian couldn't stand the sight of her, especially when she smiled. "Your Royal Highness," she began, "it pleases me to serve you –"

"Get out," he said, echoing the words he'd said to Elina. He turned away from the woman to stare at the fire, thinking of the way Elina's hair almost seemed to become alight when she was near it. It was annoyingly captivating.

"Your Royal Highness?" the woman asked uncertainly.

"I didn't stutter. Get out. I can't stand the sight of you."

She left without another word, leaving Kilian to sit, naked, in front of the fire, wondering what on earth he was doing to himself. His frustration would only grow if he left it unchecked. The tumultuous weather outside would get worse, too, though considering it remained terrible due to his constant bad mood Kilian did not care much for this point.

After a few moments he called back the servant he'd barked orders at before. "Arrange for grain, alcohol, cloth and firewood to be sent to Alder from the stores," he demanded.

"Now...?"

"In the morning, obviously!" Kilian exclaimed, beyond irritated with the servant's lack of common sense. "There's no point in having what's left of the castle's staff breaking their necks on the ice because it's pitch black outside, is there?"

"No...I'll see it done."

*I should have just fucked the prostitute,* Kilian thought grimly once the nervous servant once more left his room. But he knew that he wouldn't have been able to, even if the woman had spread herself out on his bed, wanton and lovely.

Kilian couldn't believe he had actually found a limit to his hedonistic, self-serving ways.

As with all limits imposed on him, he hated it.

# Chapter Nine

*Elina*

"Elina, you don't have to work in the shop on your day off! You must be so tired."

Elina rubbed at her eyes before giving her mother an, admittedly sleepy, smile. "I'm fine, mama. The fact you've had to work in here all by yourself whilst I've been at the castle means *you* must be tired. And you're still sick!"

Her mother laughed lightly as she carefully folded a thick, lustrous wool blanket and wrapped it in paper. "I've been much better since you started giving me those medicines from Miss Duke and Mister Wolfe."

"I still can't believe how effective everything they gave me was, to be honest."

"I suppose that's what happens when you can explore the world and pick up remedies from exotic countries. It makes sense that they'd have access to far more potent medicines."

Elina watched her mother shrewdly as Lily sat down. She'd been mentioning moving away from Alder and travelling more and more frequently with every passing day. Before, when she'd talked to Elina about seeing the world, it had been framed as an old dream - something she knew she'd never truly get to experience. But now...

*I think she might really want to leave. And if she does, and she truly is well enough to travel, then...that might just be the best thing to ever happen to us.*

For of course Elina wished to leave Alder. The only thing keeping her there was her mother and the family business. If Lily Brodeur herself was finally serious about packing up and leaving then Elina would gladly follow. Briefly she thought of her father and if he was still alive. Was it so improbable to believe that they might find the magician that had changed Lily's and, in turn, Elina's life?

Outside the shop door the ever-present sounds of blasting winds and freezing snow were engulfed by another sound entirely. Elina and her mother cocked their heads to one side in almost identical fashion, listening intently.

She glanced at her mother. "What's going on out there? It sounds like half the town are shouting." When the door to the shop was thrown open the two of them winced away from the bitter cold. "Close the door!" Elina exclaimed before she even worked out who had entered in the first place.

"Ah, my apologies Miss Brodeur!" Daven - the woodcutter - said as he struggled to close the door against the wind. Something about his tone took Elina aback. It was...genuinely conciliatory.

Lily smiled widely at Daven as he brushed snow off

his clothes and walked towards the counter. "Daven Arner. I haven't seen you in here since your mother passed. How is the family doing?"

He flashed a glance at Elina before replying, "Struggling through the winter just like everyone else, ma'am. But now it seems that's all changed for the better."

"Oh?"

Daven looked at Elina once more, this time with an incredulous grin splitting his handsome face. He had never looked at her that way, not even when they were children.

"The king has sent through supplies for the town. And - what's more - it's double what we needed, and his servant said we'll be getting more in a few weeks! Elina - Miss Brodeur - how on earth did you do it?"

Elina stared at him gawkily. "What do you mean how did I do it?"

"Oh come now, Elina!" he exclaimed, having now completely changed to addressing her informally. "Everyone knew it was a fool's errand to ask Kilian Hale for anything. But you managed to get him to send *more* than we asked for? Did you...was there magic involved?"

She rolled her eyes before she could stop herself; from her chair her mother giggled. "Mr Arner, have you ever really thought me capable of magic? If you or anybody in the town thought that then people would fear and respect me rather than ignore me."

Daven had the sense to look uncomfortable and apologetic. What surprised Elina was that the expression actually looked genuine. He ran a hand through his snow-soaked hair and looked away.

"Yes, well...I guess that's true. And it's – it's not fair that the people who ignored you were the ones who pushed you to help them."

Elina cocked an eyebrow and crossed her arms. "I seem to recall said person who pushed me into helping the town was *you.* 'Pretty enough' indeed."

Her mother burst out laughing when Daven's face turned beet red. She stood up from her chair. "Elina, if you need me I'll be in the back room starting on that jacket for Frederick."

"Mama –" Elina began, sincerely wishing not to be left alone with Daven, but her mother was already gone. She glared at Daven. "You can stop with the false gratitude now that my mother isn't around."

Daven looked ashamed. "I'm not – it isn't false gratitude. Elina, everyone is barely coping with the harsh weather. It's only because of *you* that we might pull through. I know there will always be people in Alder who won't respect or appreciate what you've done by virtue of you being, well, you, but I'm not one of them."

Shifting behind the counter and rearranging papers and ink in lieu of responding to the man, Elina was surprised when he placed his hands on top of said counter and leaned in closer to her.

"Mr Arner, what are you –"

"You didn't...you didn't go to bed with him, did you?" Daven murmured so quickly that it was clear he'd been mulling over the question for a long time.

Elina resisted the urge to slap him. "That was what everyone wanted me to do, was it not? That's what Frederick was *insinuating* at the town meeting. Does it matter how I got the prince regent to send supplies to

Alder?"

Daven looked torn. "No, I – I suppose not, but... Elina, I'm sorry. I should never have suggested you. I didn't even *want* you to do it. Not if you –"

"I didn't go to bed with Kilian Hale," Elina said flatly, brushing past Daven on her way to dust some shelves that definitely didn't need dusting. But he grabbed onto her wrist, preventing her from moving away.

"Mr –"

"You really didn't? He didn't touch you?"

Elina didn't know whether to be outraged or mortified; she settled for somewhere in the middle. "No," she said emphatically. "I don't know nor care what you think of me, nor anyone else in the town for that matter. But I care what I think about myself. And when it comes down to it, why should I bed the king for the benefit of a town that does not want me?"

"I want you."

"You – what?"

"I want you," Daven repeated, eyes bright and keen. "I always have, but I wasn't allowed. But my mother is dead, leaving me the head of my family. Nobody can tell me what I can or cannot want, now."

"The entire town would judge you."

"For what? Falling for the magician's girl who saved Alder? I think, once this winter passes, nobody will ever dare snub you, Elina."

Despite herself Elina lit up at the thought, even though she'd been relishing getting as far from the town as possible mere minutes ago. With a flick of her wrist she freed herself from Daven's grasp. "So, what you're saying is that you're only interested in me now that there's no risk to your reputation?"

"I –" Daven paused, shaking his blonde head as he laughed softly. "I guess it looks that way. But it's not really...it's not like that." He looked back up at her. "Let me take you for a drink some time. Or dinner. Let the two of us get to know one another and you can decide for yourself if my interest is superficial."

Elina clucked her tongue. "Considering how different I look from everyone in Alder I would never assume that you were even superficially interested in me."

"Elina, are you serious?" Daven stared at her as if he couldn't believe what he was hearing. "You're beautiful. And everyone knows it. It's part of the reason they hate you so."

She hadn't considered this angle before. "Why would anyone consider me beautiful when I don't conform to their standards of beauty?"

"Because pretty is pretty no matter whose *standards* you use."

Elina blushed despite herself. Aside from kind words from her grandparents and her mother she'd never received a compliment before – unless she counted the way Kilian looked at her hungrily and tried to touch himself when –

*Do not think of Kilian Hale!* she scolded herself. The last thing Kilian had intended to do was pay her a compliment when he acted the way he did. He merely viewed Elina as a plaything. Even sending the town supplies was all part of one big game he was playing with her to abate his boredom. But even so...

"I do not have much time these days for socialising, Mr Arner," Elina finally said, very carefully.

Daven's eyes grew wide. "That wasn't a no, was it? And call me Daven."

She smiled very slightly. "Not a no...Daven. But I work up at the castle most days, then help my mother out when I come back to Alder."

"You work in the castle?"

"As personal, tortured servant to the king," she said wryly. "That's how I got him to send supplies to Alder."

A flash of something Elina would, fifteen minutes ago, have never identified as jealousy crossed Daven's pale face. "You...don't need to do that for our sakes."

"Yes I do. Otherwise we'd die. I can put up with some abject humiliation for a winter – I've been doing it all my life, after all."

Daven didn't seem to know how to react to that. But then he grinned. "I go through the woods every morning looking for trees that may have been felled in the wind. Perhaps we might walk to the castle together some mornings and keep each other company?"

To Elina's surprise she actually liked the idea. Having someone to talk to that wasn't Kilian sounded like a dream. "I think I could agree to that."

"Wonderful," Daven said, still grinning. "I could pick you up from here tomorrow, then? What time must you leave?"

She grimaced. "Well before sunrise."

"Good thing I'm an early riser. I'll see you in the morning, Elina."

And with that he was gone, leaving Elina wondering what on earth had happened to her. In the space of fifteen minutes she'd been apologised to for having been ignored, thanked for everything she was doing for Alder, and confessed to for having been a man's object of desire for quite some time. She'd even agreed to something that could almost be considered courting.

All because of the whims of Kilian Hale. Elina still couldn't quite believe he'd stuck to his end of their deal.

"I have to thank him," she muttered darkly, knowing in her very soul that it was the last thing she wanted to do. But she barely had any time to mull over such an unappealing task when the door to the Brodeur shop opened once more, letting in, of all people, Adrian Wolfe.

He flashed a brilliant smile at her. "Elina Brodeur. I believe there should be a package for me."

Elina stared at him for a second too long before fumbling around the back of the counter until she located the blanket her mother had been wrapping in paper. She hadn't realised it was for Adrian but there, written on the paper, was his name. She passed it over to him demurely.

"Thank you," he said. "The tavern's rooms are awfully cold. I had it on good authority that your mother's shop was the best place for warm fabric."

She smiled at that, feeling her cheeks flush with pride. "It is, Mister Wolfe. That blanket is made of the softest, warmest wool you could find north of the equator."

Adrian considered her with interest. "Your mother

told me and Scarlett about your father, when we came in to order the blanket. So he was a foreign magician?"

Elina shrugged. "That's what my mother says, and the whole town too. I'm assuming it's why you could *smell* magic on me in the tavern."

To her surprise Adrian shook his head. "No, that doesn't explain it. The magic on you is...stronger. Constant. As if you're in contact with it all the time."

Unbidden she thought of Kilian and his empty, foreboding castle. Working up there was the only change to her life that might explain Adrian's observation, after all. But she had no proof and, even if the prince regent *was* responsible for whatever magic was clinging to her, what could Elina even do about it?

She sighed. "I guess it's a mystery, Mister Wolfe."

"Adrian," he smiled. "Just call me Adrian."

"What is it with men and demanding to be called by their first names?" she said, thinking of Daven and, of course, Kilian, whom she was yet to address in any way he actually desired.

"Because names have significance, Elina, and it's only natural when you like someone that you want them to address you in a more familiar fashion. Otherwise you may as well be strangers." Adrian gave her a wolfish grin as he made for the door. "Don't forget to stop by the tavern soon to talk with me and Scarlett - she's extremely bored."

And then Adrian wrenched open the door and was swallowed by the snow, dark cloak swirling round his ankles making him look very much the image of a mysterious magician, just like Elina used to imagine her father must have looked.

# CHAPTER TEN

***Kilian***

"Who is that man walking out of the forest with Elina?" Kilian asked the servant who was lighting the fire in his room. Though that was usually Elina's job and, indeed, the morning sky was still dark, Kilian had barely slept. He'd called the servant out of their bed to warm up his chambers and bring him wine, despite the ungodly hour. He knew why he hadn't slept, though he didn't want to confront the issue.

Kilian was supposed to have heard back from his brother by now. Gabriel and his army had to be well on course for returning from the country's borders, especially after Kilian had spoken to those diplomats. In a mere few days Gabriel was supposed to – finally – take over the throne from his younger brother.

And yet Kilian had heard nothing, and it only caused his mood to grow fouler. Watching Elina huddle next to some unknown man from Alder against the snow as she made her way to the castle didn't help.

The servant timidly approached the window to glance downward. She frowned slightly and then, with a nod of understanding, explained, "That's the woodcutter, Daven. He keeps the forest in check for the castle and builds houses in Alder."

"I thought nobody in Alder spoke to Elina..."

"Sire...?"

He waved the woman away. "You may go. What's your name?"

The servant seemed mightily surprised by this. She gulped slightly. "M-Marielle, Your Royal Highness."

"Go back to bed, Marielle. Take the morning off."

Knowing not to question this rare kindness, Marielle scurried off before Kilian could change his mind. In truth he didn't know why he'd granted her the time off. There had been something about the way she looked when she'd been hauled out of bed – like she wanted to complain about the indignity of it all but knew she couldn't – that reminded Kilian of the woman currently smiling at the woodcutter outside.

*I'm growing soft,* he thought, shivering inside his overcoat as he moved to his favourite spot by the fireplace and opened a bottle of wine. He didn't actually know what he'd say to Elina once she reached his chambers, considering how she'd left two days prior. But Kilian would be damned if he was going to let her know her rejection had any effect on him whatsoever.

"Your Royal Highness," Elina said after she knocked upon the door and entered. She was still smiling like she had done outside, with the woodcutter. Kilian hated how much it made her face glow.

"I'm assuming Alder received everything I sent

over," he murmured, not bothering to correct Elina for, once more, referring to him by his title. "Going by your expression, I mean."

To his surprise she bowed slightly. "Thank you. It's more appreciated than you could possibly know, I'd wager."

"You'd wager?"

"Yes, because you don't care."

Kilian snorted into his wine despite himself. He waved her over. "Sit down and drink with me."

"The sun hasn't even risen, Your Royal Highness."

"And considering the weather you wouldn't be able to tell if it had, anyway," he countered, gesturing towards the swirling snow dancing behind the window. "So drink with me."

Elina grimaced but, knowing she couldn't refuse, took off her cloak and placed it close to the fire to dry off. She was wearing the blue dress she'd worn when she'd originally come to beg for supplies for her stupid town - the one Kilian had first imagined removing before he'd known anything about her.

He only wanted to remove it more now that he did.

"You wear a lot of blue for someone with green eyes," he said as Elina sat as far away from Kilian on the floor as she could whilst still remaining within the fire's circle of warmth. The distance didn't go unnoticed.

She stared at him with those very eyes, expression unamused as she took the bottle of wine Kilian passed her. "I wasn't aware I was supposed to dress to match my eyes."

"That's what most women do here."

"Yes, and their eyes are blue and the clothes are blue. What a wonderful coincidence."

"Your mother runs a tailor shop. Can you not simply make your own –"

"Are you telling me you want me to wear green, Kilian?" Elina interrupted testily.

"You just said my name."

It took a few moments for Elina to realise what she'd done and then, when she did, she gulped down slightly more wine than she could handle. Spluttering and coughing, she barely managed to ask, "Do you like me, *Your Royal Highness,* or am I mere distraction?"

He shrugged, laughing as he snatched the wine back from Elina. "Both, I suppose. Does it matter?"

"It clearly doesn't matter for you, so I guess it shouldn't for me."

Elina almost seemed to sigh as she stared into the fire, the flames reflecting off her almost-black irises like a mirror. The wine had stained her lips a deep red; before Kilian could find it in him to stop himself from doing so he was staring at them.

"I'd like to see you in green, to answer your question," he said, still not tearing his eyes away from the gentle curves of Elina's lips as she softly blew a strand of hair away from her face. "Or bronze, to match your hair, and gold, to match your skin. Anything but blues and whites and greys."

When Elina finally looked at Kilian again he tore his eyes away from her. "This is coming from the man who barely manages to pull on a shirt and trousers every day, and a threadbare coat that should have been replaced years ago." She pulled at a loose thread from his sleeve to prove her point; he merely laughed at the painfully true observation. When Kilian handed over the wine once more their fingers brushed against each other.

Neither of them did anything about it.

After an hour or two Elina murmured, "It's very warm sitting so close to the fire." Kilian wasn't sure how time had passed so quickly and so easily, though the only suggestion that it had passed at all was a lightening of the white sky. There was a slight sheen on Elina's forehead - evidence that she was indeed too warm - that made her skin seem more golden and lovely that it had been before.

"So take off your clothes," Kilian joked, not expecting Elina to follow his suggestion in a thousand years. It was to his surprise, therefore, that she slowly unlaced her boots and pulled them off before sliding out of the woollen hose she wore beneath her dress. Elina's fingers then made quick work of the top portion of her dress, leaving her in a white undershirt tucked into her long, blue skirt.

"You're right," she sighed happily as she took another swig of wine, which was colouring her cheeks quicker than the fire was. "Taking off some clothes *does* feel better."

Kilian made no effort not to stare, almost wishing for the room to be cold so he could see Elina's nipples through the thin fabric of her shirt. It wouldn't take much for him to slide the sleeves down, either. All he'd have to do is reach out and -

"Your Royal Highness."

Kilian's eyes darted towards the door, the serious tone with which the interruption had been made immediately distracting him from the tantalising sight of a half-undressed Elina.

He frowned. "What is it?"

"Word from your brother."

He got to his feet immediately, not bothering to fix his hair nor put on boots before crossing his room for the door. When he saw Elina begin to stand up he waved her down. "Stay here," he ordered. "Run me a bath or something." She clearly knew better than to protest, so she demurely sat back down.

It was only once the servant had brought Kilian to his father's old strategy room that he spoke again. "What says my brother?" he demanded of the messenger who was shivering by the large, oak table etched with a map of the country and its borders. If Kilian wasn't so desperate to hear what the man had to say he might have ordered the servant to light a fire in the empty hearth.

He didn't.

"Y-Your Royal Highness," the messenger said, bowing slightly. "I come bearing unfortunate news. Your brother and his army have been delayed on the southern border, and it will take weeks for them to return."

Kilian wished he still had a wine bottle in hand simply so he could smash it. Instead he spoke very quietly, though every word was teeming with fury. "He's delayed? Why? How?"

The messenger shook his head miserably. "He would not say."

"He wouldn't *say*? He wouldn't explain his actions to his brother – his acting king? Is that what you would have me believe?"

"All he wished to relay to you was that he needed more time!"

Kilian smashed a fist against the table. "I don't *have* time to give him!"

"Sire, there is little we can do about it from here," the servant interrupted. Kilian vaguely recalled that the man had escaped being kicked out of the castle because he was one of the only servants who actually told him the truth about the things he overheard whilst working. "It would be better to send someone down to the border – to listen out for why the army is delayed."

It was a sound plan. If Gabriel didn't want Kilian to know what he was doing, then he'd have to go around him to get an answer. So Kilian nodded, the muscles in his neck and jaw so tight that he thought they might snap.

"You go for me, then. Bring someone with you. Not him," he said, gesturing towards the messenger with a flick of his head. "You have four days."

"F-four days...?"

"Ride quickly. Take my horse. *Now.*" He looked at the messenger. "And you...go back to where you came from before you went to war."

Both men left immediately without another word. Kilian paced back and forth by the table, hand to his head as he forced his brain to think. But he couldn't think. He could barely see. All he could feel was anger and –

Helplessness.

*I don't want to be here,* he thought as he left the strategy room. *I want to leave.*

# Chapter Eleven

***Elina***

Kilian was acting strangely when he finally returned to his chambers. Elina couldn't place quite what was wrong - he seemed on edge, which was strange because Kilian was never on edge. That was largely to do with the fact he was always drunk, of course, but here he was, on edge *and* drunk.

*Perhaps I'd know what was bothering him if I wasn't drunk myself,* Elina thought as she finished pouring water into the bathtub, as per Kilian's request before he'd left with his servant. She'd been drunk a handful of times in her life, though only with her mother and usually whilst playing card games or after completing particularly difficult embroidery. It felt different to be drinking with a man - especially a man she didn't like who was also her sovereign.

Elina at the very least identified that whatever was wrong with Kilian obviously had to do with his brother. *Maybe not to do with his brother and more to do with the throne,* she corrected, thinking about how little he wanted to be king. Elina had to wonder if he cared at all for his sibling, given his attitude towards everyone else.

Kilian didn't speak a word to her as he stalked back to the fireplace and sat down, a bottle of vodka in hand from which he'd already drunk a sizable quantity. Elina resisted the urge to comment on it. She badly wanted to know what news he had received about his brother and their country's army but, at the same time, Elina thought she'd rather remain ignorant. She didn't want to become any more involved in Kilian's life than she had to be.

"Your bath is ready," Elina said as she tucked away an errant lock of hair than had grown loose from her braided crown.

Kilian did not look at her. He merely stared into the fire with dispassionate eyes. It was a world away from the look on his face when he'd stared at Elina undressing.

*Only partially,* she thought, blushing for nobody to see. *I'm still mostly dressed.* But mostly dressed was still more undressed than she'd ever been in front of a man before, and having the skin of her arms and chest exposed was making Elina feel self-conscious. And yet she didn't cover up; the alcohol in her system and the heat from the fire urged her against it.

"Your Royal Highness?" she eventually said when Kilian still made no motion to move. When she'd accidentally uttered his name before, Elina realised she hadn't liked doing so at all. It made her feel too vulnerable. Kilian's official title was much safer.

*If men want me to use their first names to encourage closeness then I'd prefer to avoid them to encourage distance,* she thought, even as part of her longed for Kilian to look at her like he had done earlier. Perhaps it was because of Daven's now very obvious interest in her, sparking a desire in her to be watched and wanted, as stupid as she knew that to be.

"You –"

"I heard you the first time."

Elina was struck by how flat Kilian's voice was. Uncertainly she took a few steps towards him, her bare feet soft and silent on the large, luxurious rug that sat in front of the fire. The air was full of steam from the bath, spicy and heady and fragrant. She inhaled it deeply before speaking again.

"What news did you receive from your brother, if you don't mind me asking?"

It took Kilian a while to respond. He swigged from his vodka bottle several times; Elina saw that his hand was shaking. Looking even closer she saw the muscles of his neck were bunched and tight – far worse than they had been when she'd massaged them two days ago.

"Gabriel and the army are delayed in the south," Kilian finally said. "For weeks at least. He didn't deign to tell me why."

"That's – these things happen. It's war. I'm sure there's –"

"If there's a reasonable explanation then Gabriel would have seen fit to tell me. He simply doesn't want to return."

Elina frowned. "Why would that be the case? When he comes back he'll –"

"Be king. I know. That's why."

"He doesn't wish to be king?" she asked, torn between curiosity and a burning desire to simply leave the conversation before finding out any more.

"I don't know," Kilian said simply, swirling the contents of the bottle in his hands round and round even as he looked as if he sincerely wished to smash it.

Elina tried to feign a smile. "If you don't know then perhaps you should find out."

"Do you not think I know that already? Or do you believe me to be stupid?"

"I – no. I suppose I don't."

He glared at her. "You *suppose*?"

In her drunk boldness Elina decided to speak her mind. "It's hardly as if you've given me much evidence either way. Other than your obvious cruelty and general disrespect for your country I hardly know anything about you."

Kilian's eyes flashed as he stood up and rounded on Elina. She held her ground, though she desperately wanted to take a step back.

"I don't understand you, Elina. You say you hate Alder, and with good reason. You could leave at any moment – literally any given moment – and improve your circumstances elsewhere, and yet you don't."

Elina frowned. "What's your point?"

"I would *kill* to be in your position – to have that opportunity to simply up and leave with a puff of smoke like that magician father of yours."

"Then leave."

"I can't!"

"Then you're no different than me, who won't leave Alder!" she exclaimed. "You say you don't care about anyone but clearly, deep down, you must do. There's some sense of responsibility in you that knows you have to look after –"

Kilian grabbed her arms with such ferocity that Elina took a step back; he followed. "You weren't listening to me," he growled. "I. Can't. Leave."

For the first time since Elina met Kilian she had to admit she was frightened of him. His fingers on her arms were like steel, bruising her skin even as she stood there. Pale, tangled hair was wild around his face; his even paler eyes aflame whilst he breathed heavily and his overcoat slipped from his shoulders.

Kilian looked mad – downright insane – and it was in that very moment Elina realised he quite possibly always had been.

"What do you mean you can't?" she whispered, too afraid to raise her voice.

"It means exactly that," Kilian said, unblinking. "It means that my father, on his deathbed, knew that Gabriel had to go to war and that someone needed to sit on the throne whilst he was gone. It means that my father also knew his second son would never do it, because said second son would rather spend his days in a foreign whorehouse drinking wine until he died. It means that my father subsequently knew he had to tie that son to the throne."

Elina didn't say anything. She merely stood there, trapped by Kilian's vice-like grip, until he spoke again. He laughed bitterly. "Your father really did gift mine with magic all those years ago, when the winter was so bad it would put this one to shame. To him the spell that was cast was a blessing; I always thought it a curse."

"'You can control the weather of your country,' your father said, "with your heart and soul you will control the weather. You will become your country and your country will be you.' I was only three and yet I remember it word for word. It was terrifying, you see. Gabriel would agree with me, if you were to ask him in private."

Kilian finally let go of Elina to pick up his forgotten bottle of vodka and took a long draught of it, then thrust it out towards her. "Drink," he demanded.

"I -"

"That was an order."

So Elina drank, wincing at the burn in her throat as she swallowed the liquid. She took a careful step or two away from Kilian for fear that he would grab her again, but he didn't. He ran his hands through his long, tangled hair until his face was clear of it. In the firelight he looked gaunt and hollow; his cheekbones too well-defined and his jawline too sharp. Elina wondered when he'd last eaten properly.

"There were conditions to your father's magic, as there always are with these things," he said quietly. He glanced at Elina as he brought a hand up in front of his face, counting down each condition on his fingers as he spoke them. "One: the king - my father - could not leave the castle. The spell was tied quite literally to who sat on the throne. Two: the weather was linked to the king's mood. If he was happy and gentle then the winds and sun and snow would reflect this. If he was...less so, the weather would be harsh and stormy." Kilian paused, taking a breath before continuing. "And three: the spell *must* be passed on to the blood relative who succeeds the throne."

Elina's brain was numb. She couldn't possibly take in all of this information, not least when she was drunk and terrified. "...why did your father agree to the spell?" she found herself asking, though she didn't know where she found the strength to speak.

Kilian rolled his eyes. "The man was a fool. He loved his country, and everyone in it. He happily agreed to such stupid terms. And my mother...she was already ill, so she couldn't leave the castle anyway. He thought giving up his freedom was a small price to pay to be a good king. And he was, of course." Kilian looked out of the window, where the wind was howling so loudly it was if it wanted to scream at him. "My father was a good king – even I can admit that. He was calm, trustworthy and quick to love. You know how short and mild our winters have been. That was his doing."

Even though it felt rather like approaching a starving bear or wolf or mountain cat, Elina took a few tentative steps towards Kilian. He didn't look at her. "So he... passed the spell to you?"

"Against my will," he muttered, staring at the floor. "In the dead of night, when I should have been asleep but was, in reality, too drunk to even be unconscious, he loomed over my bed and cursed me to stay."

"Your father...he died in September?"

Kilian nodded. "He cursed me in summer, though, before Gabriel left. Clearly he knew I planned to run off. But because he still sat on the throne until his death, I didn't inherit his *powers* until autumn."

"That would explain this god-awful winter," Elina muttered despite herself.

She regretted it immediately. Kilian whipped around and grabbed her once more, pushing her backwards until her legs slammed against the bathtub.

"Is this a joke to you?!" he screamed right to her face. "Am *I* a joke to you?"

"No, I –"

"Because that's what it seems like. No, that's what it *is* like – with everyone. You think I don't know what people say about Kilian Hale, the king they never wanted? The king they hope disappears? The king they expect to fail, so god only hopes that his saintly brother Gabriel returns from the war soon, right?"

"I didn't say anything like that!" Elina protested, though of course she was guilty of having such thoughts on numerous occasions. But that had been *before* she knew why Kilian didn't simply do everyone a favour and leave. Of course things were different now she knew.

And yet the person standing in front of her was nevertheless frightful and intimidating. Elina tried to lean away as much as she could; Kilian responded by picking her up and throwing her into the steaming bath.

"See, even you shy away from me and you're my *servant*!" he seethed, hands curled around the edge of the tub as Elina spluttered and choked on murky, salty water.

When she finally regained her breath enough to meet Kilian's gaze there were tears in her eyes. "I am not your servant," she said. "I never have been."

"Of course you are! Why else would you be here?!"

"Because you blackmailed me!" Elina cried out. When she tried to get out of the bath Kilian reached out and stopped her from doing so with a heavy hand on her chest. She continued to struggle nonetheless, water soaking through every inch of fabric clinging to her skin. "You wouldn't have helped Alder if I hadn't –"

"You really think I'd have let the town die?! Do you honestly believe I could have looked out of my window and watch people literally starve to death when there's enough in the castle stores to help them through seven winters, Elina?"

"Then why did you force me to –"

"Because I was lonely!" Kilian didn't seem to be aware of what he was saying. His fingers curled around Elina's shirt; he bent down until his head was just above hers, eyes wild and and angry and so bitterly sad that Elina realised she'd been a fool not to see how Kilian had felt before.

"You – why didn't you simply ask me to keep you company, then?" Elina asked quietly.

Kilian choked on a laugh that sounded more like a sob. "And would you have said yes?"

"...no."

"Then you see my problem."

"Ask me again."

Kilian blinked. He narrowed his eyes. "What do you mean?"

"Ask me again to keep you company."

There was a pause. Kilian looked at her, and Elina looked at him, and their eyes gave absolutely nothing away to the other.

"You..." Kilian murmured, voice barely audible over the storm outside that was his very own doing. "Will you keep me company?"

Elina tilted her head up, snaking a hand behind Kilian's neck before she could stop herself. She pulled his lips to hers.

“Yes.”

# Chapter Twelve

*Kilian*

How had the events of the day culminated in such a moment – Elina's dark, wine-stained lips willingly pressed to his? Kilian's mind went blank. For one, blind moment, there was nothing. His body wouldn't move. Wouldn't react. And then –

Kilian reciprocated Elina's kiss with a ferocity and passion he hadn't felt in a long, long time. He collapsed into the bath with her, not caring for the water he displaced to the floor, drenching the rugs and wooden boards in one fell splash.

He couldn't get close enough, nor could he get his hands through Elina's hair – her braided crown was secured far too tightly to her scalp. So Kilian made do with straddling her lap, bending low to deepen their kiss until he leaned back with enough force to pull Elina on top of him in a wave of steaming bathwater.

Kilian closed his eyes to protect from the sting of the salt in the water; when he opened them a somewhat dazed and heavy-lidded Elina was pressed against him, hands still entwined in his hair as she finally pulled her lips away from his.

"What was that for?" Kilian asked, hating himself for even asking the question when the mood had suddenly – finally – become good enough for him to find himself in such a suggestive situation with Elina.

Elina didn't look away as she replied, "Because you were right. I thought you a joke. Everyone else still does. Now, knowing the truth and...actually *looking* at you properly, I..." She paused, as if deciding whether she should utter her next sentence. "You're pathetic, Kilian Hale, but for the first time in my life I now know that it's not *all* your fault."

Kilian stared at her, too stunned to speak. When he burst out laughing he surprised even himself, considering how dark and angry he'd been mere moments before. He slid a hand down Elina's back, fingering the waistband of her skirt until he found the buttons that would loosen it. Elina's eyes darted downward when he proceeded to remove the material, her face red from heat and alcohol and embarrassment.

"So you kissed me because I'm pathetic?" he murmured, finally pulling the length of Elina's skirt from her body and tossing the drenched material unceremoniously to the floor. Her white undershirt barely covered her body to her thighs; soaked through as it was it hardly hid anything at all. "How pathetic do I need to be for those hands of yours to wander downward, Elina?"

He was gratified when the flush of her cheeks crawled across her ears and down her neck. "I – I never said I *kissed* you because you were pathetic. Only that you're pathetic in general."

"Oh? Then why, specifically, did you kiss me?" Kilian asked, placing his hands over Elina's to guide them down from his hair, across his chest and to his navel.

"I - because..." she hesitated. Her hands wrung the edge of Kilian's shirt nervously beneath the water's surface; he was aching for her to move them further down. "Truthfully, I'm not sure," Elina finally answered. "I don't even think I like you."

Kilian chuckled, urging Elina's lips back to his own for another kiss. He slid his tongue into her mouth, running it across the edge of her teeth before biting gently down onto her lower lip.

"It doesn't seem to matter whether you like me or not, going by the situation we're currently in."

"Kilian."

He paused abruptly at the sound of his name which he, aside from her having mistakenly uttered it earlier, hadn't heard spoken by another person since before his father died.

"What is it?"

Elina looked a little uncertain. Kilian's hands found her thighs, repositioning the woman on top of him until she was properly sitting on the aching pit of frustration that had left him hard after most every encounter with her over the past week. She cried out in surprise.

"What did you - ah - stop trying to pleasure yourself when I'm speaking to you," she complained when Kilian rocked her against him; a low groan whistled between his teeth at the sensation.

"Do a better job of speaking, then," he replied, hands roaming up beneath Elina's shirt even as he fumbled to hold a coherent train of thought.

"You said you liked me earlier. But is that simply because you're lonely? Is it because there's no one else? Is – this – because there's no one else?"

To that, Kilian could only laugh. "Elina, I'm sure you remember what happened two nights ago. Considering you were sober and I was wasted, I imagine you remember it much better than I do, in fact."

She frowned. "What are you getting at?"

Kilian sighed when he moved Elina against him once more, hands on her waist inexorably climbing upwards even as Elina watched him do so nervously.

"I called for a prostitute to be brought to my chambers as soon as you left," he explained, so off-handedly that it took a moment for Elina to realise what he'd said. When she did she tried to recoil, but Kilian only pulled her closer against him. His lips found her collarbone, trailing kisses across her wet skin. Beneath his mouth Elina was trembling; Kilian only wanted her more as a result.

"When the woman arrived I couldn't stand to look at her," he continued, his words barely a mumble against Elina's chest. "All I could think of was you. I sent her away – I, Kilian Hale, sent a prostitute away. Unheard of. So to answer your question, Elina Brodeur..."

He glanced upwards at Elina, her eyes glittering and dark as she stared back at him. "I don't just like you because I'm lonely. Granted that's how I got to know you, but that's not why I like you. And it's certainly not why I'm physically attracted to you – I've wanted to bed you from the moment I saw you. But you already knew that."

"You saw me as an object," she replied, turning her head away until Kilian used a hand to make her look at him once more. "Viewing me like that is different from being attracted to me for *me*."

"I guess that's true. Which leads me to ask: though you profess not to like me, are you nonetheless attracted to *me* for me? Or are you, in your own words, viewing me as an object right now?"

Kilian glanced very pointedly downward; the meaning was not lost on Elina.

"I don't - I've never viewed you as anything less than a person."

"Merely a pathetic one."

"I - yes. And a cruel one. And a lazy one."

"And yet here we are."

Kilian kissed her before Elina could construct a response, and this time her hands moved on their own. They ran beneath his shirt, fingers gliding over soaking, slippery skin without quite touching Kilian where he was dying for her to.

When his own hands finally crept over Elina's breasts he paused, and pulled his lips away slightly from hers. "Nobody has ever touched you like this before, have they?"

She shook her head. "Nobody."

"Have you ever imagined someone touching you like this?"

"I - no. There's no man in Alder I could imagine ever *wanting* to touch me."

Kilian found this deeply sad and frustrating. How could an entire town be so narrow-minded simply because a baby was born a bastard to a foreigner? He wondered how the people of Alder would react to the dark-skinned people Kilian had met on his travels across other continents. Not well, he imagined.

"They are all fools," he said with surety, for of course they were. Except the woodcutter, who was a threat for Kilian to consider when he was not half-naked in a bath with the woman he so desired.

Elina laughed softly. "I know they are."

"When you go to bed tonight, will you think of me touching you?"

"When I...go to bed?"

Kilian nodded and, though he hated himself and his body was screaming at him not to do it, gently moved Elina away from his lap. "You are drunk. As much as I want this to continue, if I'm to prove I actually respect you then...we can continue this sober."

Elina's eyes widened in disbelief. "You're *always* drunk, Kilian. I doubt you're even sober in your sleep."

"I can't argue with that," he chuckled, hands reaching out for Elina even as he tried to resist doing so. "But from tomorrow I will be. Though god knows if either of us will like who I am sober."

She quirked an eyebrow. "I don't even like you as you are now, remember?"

"It's very quiet outside."

Elina seemed taken aback by the sudden change in topic. She cocked her head to the side to listen, a motion so irresistible that Kilian reached for her beneath the water's surface despite himself.

"You're right," she said. "It's quiet outside. I assumed..."

"You assumed what?"

Elina blushed. "I assumed the weather would get rather wild if you were – you know –"

"If I was half-naked in a bathtub with a beautiful woman?"

She nodded whilst Kilian laughed. "It was certainly bad enough after you left the other night. And I'll admit to having seriously considered stranding you here by getting in as tempestuous a mood as possible."

"*Kilian*!"

"I do love it when you say my name. At least I didn't though. That ought to count for something."

The look on Elina's face suggested she didn't entirely agree with this.

Kilian relaxed his head against the bath, content to watch Elina sitting mostly naked on top of his legs. "I definitely want to fuck you right now," he said, so casually that Elina almost choked in shock. "But I'm... okay with knowing I won't. That I can wait until a better time. When my head doesn't feel...cloudy. I don't know. It feels nice, though a certain part of me doesn't agree with that."

Elina's hands grazed against that *certain part* as if to affirm what Kilian was saying. He was gratified to see her gulp somewhat. And then he sighed, shaking water from his hair as he finally pulled himself out of the bath.

"I really need to sober up fast," he mused, mostly to himself, shedding his sodden clothes and wrapping himself in a large robe before finding one for Elina.

"I think this is the most modesty you've ever demonstrated to me, *Your Royal Highness,*" she said coyly, placing the robe over her shoulders before hurriedly sliding out of her shirt. Kilian deliberately turned away, not entirely trusting his self-control to see Elina truly naked.

"Very funny. You're welcome to stay in the castle, of course, since your clothes are soaking –"

"Are there any servant's clothes I can borrow?" Elina asked instead as she wrung out her skirt. Kilian couldn't help but feel disappointed. He'd half-hoped she would want to stay in bed with *him.*

"I – don't see why not."

She smiled. "Thank you. My mother will be worried if I don't come home."

Kilian glanced out of the window. "It's still early, you know. Barely past lunchtime."

"Then I can tell her you were so magnanimous as to allow me a half-day because the weather turned fair. It might go a long way in making me like you."

He caught Elina's wrist and pulled her in against him. "That's not fair," he said, lips grazing her jaw as he spoke. "You could hold something like that over me for the rest of my life."

"Would that really be so bad? To have an annoying, human, moral compass?"

"That sounds terrible. That's the worst idea I've ever heard."

When Elina brushed her lips against Kilian's he knew it was time to say good-bye. "I'll find some servant's clothes myself," she said, "and then I'll be on my way. Have fun sobering up, Kilian."

"I'm still inclined to set a storm upon you the moment you set foot outside!" he called out after her once she'd strode across the room and opened the door.

"I don't doubt that. But if you want me back tomorrow then you won't."

And so Kilian had no choice but to let her leave. Grimacing at the feeling of walking on a rug drenched in cold water, he located his half-empty bottle of vodka and smashed it into the fireplace.

Part of him regretted it immediately.

# Chapter Thirteen

*Elina*

"Elina, wait up!"

Elina glanced over her shoulder to see Daven racing to catch up with her. She stopped and smiled, though inside she wanted to run off to be alone. She had so much to think about, after all.

Too much, possibly. And she was still drunk.

Daven eyed her curiously when he finally reached her side. "Elina, why is your hair so wet? And are you in different clothes than you were wearing this morning?" he asked when her cloak shifted enough for him to see beneath it.

"The regent - ah - had a bit of a tantrum in the bath," Elina explained, for the first time in her life feeling a twinge of guilt about bad-mouthing Kilian Hale. Though what she was saying wasn't a lie, so to speak. It simply wasn't the whole truth, either.

"He shouldn't be having you bathe him," Daven

bristled. "Surely he must have other servants who can do that. This isn't fair on you."

Elina shrugged as they continued through the murky forest, which was eerie in its stillness. She hadn't realised just how accustomed to the stormy weather she'd gotten.

*How much I've become used to Kilian's foul moods, more like,* she thought, smiling slightly at the thought. Though what had happened to Kilian was horrific - tragic, even - knowing that *she* affected his mood to the point of influencing the weather was... satisfying. Or exciting. Or terrible. Elina thought her feelings on the matter were probably somewhere in the middle.

"Elina, are you okay?" Daven asked, abruptly bringing her back into the present.

She laughed softly. "I'm fine. More than fine, really. I'm glad to have a half-day. I can help my mother out for a while."

"Ah, might I be able to interest you in coming for a drink in Gill's tavern? I don't want to push you, just... you said you didn't have much time because of working at the castle, so..."

Maybe it was because of the alcohol still in her system, or Elina's desire to show off to the people of Alder that she'd managed to do exactly what they thought she couldn't, but she nodded her head. "I'd be happy to, Daven."

It rather seemed that Daven himself was the happy one upon hearing her response. He walked her straight to the front door of her mother's tailor shop and even then seemed reluctant to part. But eventually he did, with promises to see her in the tavern after dinner, and

Elina entered the shop much to Lily's surprise.

"Elina!" she cried out. "I was not expecting you back so soon. Are you - have you been drinking? What happened to you?"

Elina could only laugh. Or course her mother could tell that she was drunk. "It's a...story for another time," she said, "when I know a little more about it myself. I'm going to change and fix my hair then I'll come back and help you out."

Her mother *tsked.* "You absolutely will not. Go to sleep and sober up. Heaven knows you could do with the sleep, anyway."

"Dutifully noted. And..." Elina glanced at the front door. "I may be going to the tavern tonight for a drink, if that's okay."

"Are you meeting Daven?"

Elina blushed. "How did you know?"

"Oh come now," her mother laughed. "I've always known the boy had his eye on you. Nice to see he finally plucked up the courage to talk to you."

"I - how did you know *that?* I never saw him looking at me!"

The look on Lily's face was entirely sympathetic as she surveyed her daughter. "Of course you didn't. He only looked when you couldn't see. *I* saw, though."

"Why didn't you say anything?"

"Would it have changed your circumstances in Alder if you knew? We both know it wouldn't. I didn't want to hurt you more than I already have by telling you about people who wanted to get to know you but couldn't."

"I..." Elina reached her mother's side and held her

hand. "You have never hurt me, mama."

"I have; you've merely lived with it every day of your life so you cannot see it. Things would be different for you if you were –"

"Don't you dare say 'if I was like everyone else'. I don't need that, mama. I like who I am, and if the rest of the town are only acknowledging me now that I've helped them when nobody else could then that's on them, not you or me."

It was only in saying it that Elina realised it was true. She'd always wanted to be part of the town before – to look like them and laugh with them. But now she knew better. There was a world outside of Alder, even if she'd never seen it, and the opinions of one town meant little and less in the grand scheme of things.

*Especially when the 'grand scheme of things' involves curses and weather magic and trapping a king in a castle.*

Because that was the truth of it; Elina's problems were tiny compared to Kilian's. They didn't even matter. No wonder he'd been so disinterested in her 'sob story', as he'd put it, when they'd first met. Because Elina *could* leave at any point, really; it was fear holding her back.

Kilian couldn't so much as step a foot outside of his castle.

"Elina? Do you feel ill? Did you drink too much?"

She blinked, then shook her head as she smiled. "No, mama. I just have...a lot to think about. I'll go and sleep."

"I am so proud of you. Keep working hard and then, when winter is over, let's leave Alder for good."

Elina had never given her mother a proper answer when she'd talked about leaving before. This time, she did.

"Absolutely. Spring can't come quickly enough."

*

When Elina arrived in Gill's tavern she was decidedly sober and full of nerves. She'd considered letting her hair hang loose but, as expected, she was too much of a coward to do it, even though she had decided hours before that she didn't care about fitting into Alder anymore. So her hair remained braided around her head, and she wore an inoffensive, dove-grey dress that nevertheless stood out for how finely made it was. Elina had made it herself, in truth, though the town did not know how talented she was. They only bought products her mother made, after all.

"Elina, over here!" Daven called out when he spied her. Nervously she made her way through the throng of thirsty tavern-goers, painfully aware of everyone's eyes on her. When she sat down Daven immediately handed her a tankard of ale, though she'd never drank the stuff before.

"A toast to Prince Kilian for providing us with the alcohol we're drinking, and to Miss Brodeur for wrangling it out of him!" he announced. To Elina's surprise people *actually* cheered for this, even though it meant cheering for her.

And then she was bombarded by conversation after conversation - answering more questions and speaking to more people than she ever had in her life. To her right Daven sat proudly, which didn't seem to be disingenuous at all. He *was* proud of her.

She wondered how proud of her he'd be if he knew what she'd been up to that morning.

*Don't think about Kilian,* Elina thought. Now was not the time. When she was back in her bed, alone, she could think about him. But even that caused her to blush. *He was the one who told me to think about him in bed, though he definitely didn't mean for me to mull over his problems.*

But how could she not? Now that Elina's own, highly insignificant, problem seemed to have been solved, she wanted to help him. She wanted to free Kilian from his prison.

A lustrous wave of dark hair by the stairs alerted Elina to the fact that Scarlett had come down to the tavern floor. Adrian wasn't with her. When Elina caught her eye the woman smiled, but shook her head as an indication for Elina not to join her. It sent a shiver up Elina's spine; what was going on?

*Should I tell Scarlett and Adrian about Kilian's curse?*

Of course Elina wanted to – how else could she help him, after all? But it wasn't her secret to share. She didn't have the right to talk to other people about it. And yet even so...

"Elina, did your mother make your dress?" a young woman around Elina's age asked, bringing her back out of her head. "It's gorgeous!"

"It's soft as sin, too," Daven added on, stroking a finger up the sleeve as if touching Elina was the most natural thing in the world. Again, she thought of Kilian, and how it felt like electricity was running through her whenever he touched her. She had wanted to run away from getting shocked just as badly as she yearned for the feeling. Daven's touch wasn't like that. It felt familiar and safe, though in truth they'd only been speaking to each other for two days.

"I made it, actually," Elina said bashfully, to the sound of a dozen envious cries.

"You must make me one in blue!"

"I want one with flowers embroidered in the bodice for spring!"

"Can you make an overcoat this soft?"

The comment gave Elina an unexpected flash of inspiration. Though she couldn't hope to help Kilian with breaking his curse on her own, she *could* do something about him always being cold.

And she could start with the ragged, threadbare excuse for an overcoat he practically lived in.

# Chapter Fourteen

***Kilian***

Kilian had never been so cold. Which was saying something, because he was almost always cold. But without alcohol in his system to fool his brain into thinking he was warm he couldn't stop shaking. His body was wracked with painful jerks and shivers that set his teeth on edge.

His head was killing him, too; he'd never had so painful and so constant a migraine before. He had no appetite and, when he *did* eat, it wasn't long before he simply threw the food back up. A fever had broken across his brow which, even when setting him on fire, altogether felt like he'd been plunged into a biting lake of ice water.

But Kilian was no idiot. He knew he deserved each and every inch of pain his body was currently experiencing. It was a just punishment for keeping himself inebriated for the past nine of his twenty-five pitiful years. His system literally did not know how to cope without any alcohol. Dully he thought about calling the doctor in to help him only to remember that he'd fired the man for so unfairly allowing his father to die.

*I am a horrible person,* he thought, brain rattling in his skull as he shivered beneath several blankets on his bed. *It's no wonder nothing's happened with Elina since she got drunk with me.*

This wasn't strictly the reason, of course. For the past few days Kilian had been so ill and barely-conscious that he'd pushed Elina to help the other servants in the castle instead of looking after him. But still. He'd hoped she'd insist on waiting on him every moment of every day anyway, rather than take him up on his offer to leave him alone.

For Kilian was miserable alone. And he'd always been alone, so he was always miserable. It was only in meeting Elina that he could even acknowledge this, however, since to admit to being lonely was pitiable.

*Yet despite calling me pathetic Elina is still here.*

Kilian was ashamed by his drunken admission of loneliness to her, especially since she'd had no trouble expressing the same feelings to him from the very beginning with regards to the people of Alder. He'd never felt so dishonest.

"Shut up, brain..." he mumbled, groaning as he twisted in bed. It didn't do well to think about the person he'd become after all these years. And it wasn't as if Kilian had drastically changed in personality when he'd started drinking; he had always been an unpleasant person. Elina's mother, Lily, would be able to attest to that, from when she watched in horror as three-year-old Kilian burned the clothes she'd so carefully made for him.

He was a snob. He was bad-tempered. He had a superiority complex a mile high. He was impulsive and cowardly and cruel-tongued and –

"I want Elina."

The words were barely a puff of breath upon the air in his room. Though the fire was burning brightly, Kilian's chambers felt like ice. Or, rather, Kilian himself felt like he was made of ice, in a furnace that could never melt him.

He was so cold.

Kilian could only really tell what time of day it was by when he spied Elina arriving at the castle in the morning, since when he wasn't lying in bed he was collapsed by his window, watching the wind relieve the forest of snow only for more to replace it.

She was almost always accompanied by the woodcutter, Daven, though occasionally another person or two decided to join their morning walk even though the weather was horrific and the hour ungodly. The fact that it was always *men* talking to Elina only served to make Kilian's mood worse – was she so oblivious as to not understand what they were interested in? It was clear as day from where Kilian sat, watching, even through the snow.

But Elina seemed to be enjoying the company. He couldn't help but wonder if, now she had been accepted by her town, she was no longer interested in Kilian, no matter how reluctant that interest had been in the first place. He had to remind himself that he'd forced Elina to get drunk the day she kissed him and they ended up in the bath together. Even Kilian could see how her actions could be explained as being the result of coercion rather than being voluntary.

It only made him feel worse.

Even though it was definitely colder outside than in his room he longed to be down there, amongst the swirling snow. He'd always hated the castle grounds before - for no reason whatsoever other than Kilian hated everything - but now they were tantalising. He couldn't set foot in the gardens, or the courtyard, or the forest. He couldn't use the hot springs, the only part of the castle and its grounds he would ever profess to enjoying.

He couldn't show Elina around all the places he used to hide from his parents and brother, or the spot in the forest where he'd disappear to with a stolen bottle of wine even as young as thirteen. Kilian had never wanted to tell anyone about his childhood before. And, now that he did, Elina didn't seem to be interested enough to listen to him talk about it. Kilian didn't like how that made him feel at all.

Rolling around in bed to try and untangle himself from a blanket currently wound around his leg, Kilian yelped in surprise when he accidentally overshot the movement and ended up on the floor. When he bashed his head upon the wooden floorboards his vision went white, then black.

*

When he came to, Kilian was still lying on the floor exactly where he'd fallen, feeling even worse than he had felt before. His head felt like it was going to split open, but when he retched nothing came out. There was nothing left for him *to* throw up.

The room was almost dark; the fire had burned low and the sun - wherever it had been behind the clouds - had clearly long since set.

*I can't believe I knocked myself out for hours by falling out of bed,* Kilian thought, laughing bitterly. But the only audible sound that left his mouth was a garbled cry; fumbling in the darkness he reached for a metal pitcher of water that sat on a table by his bedside. When he poured the stinging, freezing liquid down his throat more of it escaped his mouth than was swallowed, leaving trails of ice water running down his neck.

He wished the water were vodka. Or wine. Or ale, which he hated. He couldn't stand the pain of merely existing anymore. And so Kilian staggered to his feet, clutching his well-worn overcoat around himself as he tried desperately to find any kind of alcohol whatsoever in his room. When no bottles became immediately apparent, he began pushing chairs over and knocking down tables, smashing ornaments and vases to the floor in his quest to find something that would numb his existence.

There was nothing.

All he had to do was call for a servant and Kilian would be handed over anything he so desired. But if he did that then he knew he'd truly failed, and he'd never be able to stop drinking until his sorry excuse for a life was well and truly spent.

Kilian sagged against the window. For there was his answer - he *couldn't* drink, even if he found some irresistible volume of alcohol hidden away in a corner of his room that he was yet to upturn. He had to endure the unendurable until he was no longer in pain.

"How long will that be?" Kilian sighed, voice weak and insubstantial as he shivered violently. He didn't even have the capacity to shout for a servant, much less Elina, and he was the one who'd told them all to leave him alone. Kilian's solitude was his own damn fault, and he knew it.

In a moment of madness he undid the latch on his window, hauling open the man-sized panes of glass until he could stand on the window ledge and feel the full force of the wind buffet his entire body. It should have been strong enough to drag Kilian off the ledge and down, down, down to his death.

But he could not leave the castle, so the wind did nothing to him.

He was ashamed when tears began to well up in his eyes. Kilian wasn't even sure he *wanted* to die. He was certainly too much of a coward to run a blade through his heart or slit his throat or swallow poison or even let himself freeze to death. But falling through the window into a storm of his own making...

There was something poetic and circular about it, like it was the way Kilian was supposed to die. Except that he couldn't. Maybe that was why he liked it; it was something he could never have.

"Oh my god - Kilian!"

Elina slammed into his back and wrapped her arms around his waist, dragging him away from the window ledge as far as she could. Kilian didn't even resist.

"What were you - why were you doing that?" she asked, voice hysterical as she continued to cling to him. Elina was warm and Kilian freezing; he relished the embrace.

"I wasn't doing anything," he said weakly, which was technically the truth.

"Don't lie to me! You think I can't work out what you were -"

"I can't leave the castle, Elina. If I was going to kill myself it wouldn't be by jumping out of the window."

"That...that sounds like you tried, to see if it was possible."

Kilian didn't respond, confirming Elina's suspicions. He didn't want to turn around and face her when he still had tears in his eyes. But he was shivering so badly, and he hardly felt able to support his own weight.

"Kilian, why did you - why would you tell me to work with the other servants when you're like this?" Elina asked quietly. With utmost care she took a step backwards and, when Kilian followed, another, and another, until they reached his bed. Then she let go of him, shaking out and rearranging the pile of blankets upon it before gently pushing Kilian on top of them.

"Get in there. Now. I'm going to get the fire going again and bring you food, and you're *going to eat it.*" In the darkness she couldn't see his tears or, if she could, Elina didn't acknowledge them.

He stared at her, helpless. "I can't keep anything down. I can't feel anything except the cold, even in my stomach. It hurts, Elina."

Her expression crumpled. "Then why would you tell me not to look after you? I could have helped you!"

"I..." Kilian looked away. "I wanted you to insist on looking after me yourself. I wanted it to be your choice."

"Are you an *idiot*?!" she yelled, stepping forward as if to slap him but tripping on a box Kilian had thrown to the floor instead. She cursed aloud. "What did you do to your room? Why are you like this? Why are you –"

"I don't know what to do with myself. I want to die."

"No you don't." Elina's eyes were shining in the darkness, overly bright and, Kilian realised, just as teary as his own were. "You don't want to die. You're going through withdrawal. You're starving. You're freezing. But you've been struggling through it for days now – if you wanted to die you'd have done it already."

Kilian said nothing. He didn't know *what* to say. He was so tired of everything, but he knew he couldn't sleep.

Elina sighed. "Get in bed. I'll sort everything out. Just...try and get warm."

And so Kilian complied, crawling beneath the covers whilst watching Elina struggle to close the window, start up a new fire until it was roaring, then ask a servant to bring through some food. She didn't try to clean up properly, merely pushing away things on the floor into the corners so that she wouldn't trip.

When the servant brought through a bowl of soup and some bread they didn't question the mess of the king's chambers, nor the state of the man himself. They merely handed Elina the food and ran off.

She perched herself on the bed, glancing at Kilian from beneath her lashes. "Sit up, Kilian. You can't eat lying down."

"I already told you, I can't keep any food –"

"Sit. Up."

He wasn't used to being ordered around. For a moment he considered chastising Elina for having the audacity to do so. Instead, he complied. "Are you going to feed me?" he asked, some of his usual sarcastic way of speaking finally returning.

When Elina nodded seriously and immediately

shoved a spoonful of soup into his mouth Kilian was too surprised to retort. "I'm not going to stop until you're done with the whole thing," she said, bringing another spoonful of soup up for Kilian to drink as soon as he'd swallowed the first one.

Twenty minutes passed in this fashion, during which time the fire began to properly heat up the room. But Kilian was still so cold, and the pain in his head was yet to abate. When he winced in response to it, Elina brought out a small vial of powder from a pocket of her dress, pouring it into a cup of water before handing it to Kilian.

He stared at the cup dubiously. "What are you giving me?"

"Powdered willow bark. You should have been taking it for the pain already."

"I don't need something like that to -"

"I'm not going to listen to a man who drinks his pain away tell me he doesn't want to take medicine that will do the same thing."

This version of Elina was ruthless. But Kilian realised it was what he needed, so he swallowed down the water in one go.

Finally she smiled. "Good. Keep sitting until that hits you, then lie down and go to sleep."

"You're not - don't go, Elina."

Kilian hated how desperate he sounded.

Elina moved the now-empty tray of food onto the only table that Kilian hadn't upturned. "I won't," she said quietly. "The weather is too bad for me to leave, anyway. You *did* say you wanted to trap me here, before;

I should have expected this."

"I didn't –"

"I know you can't help it," she cut in. "You're in pain. It's okay. I'll help you through it, so just focus on not being sick."

He laughed weakly. "Easy for you to say. You're not the one who feels like this."

"True; I merely have to be able to stomach looking after you like this."

"Please stop making cruel jokes; it hurts to laugh."

Elina's lips quirked at the comment. "Noted. Close your eyes, Kilian. Just try and relax."

It was easier said than done. Even when the willow bark took the pain away from his head and settled his stomach, finally allowing him to keep down food for the first time in days, he was still cold. Too cold. The shivering wouldn't stop. Kilian sank below the covers, wondering how he would ever sleep.

"Elina," he said some time later, keeping his eyes closed so he wouldn't see her reaction when she invariably rejected him.

"...yes?"

"Lie in bed with me. Keep me warm."

She was supposed to say no. Any sane person would have said no.

"Okay."

# Chapter Fifteen

***Elina***

"Okay?"

"That's what I said."

In truth Elina was terrified. She had no idea why she'd agreed to such a proposal, not least when Kilian was in such a state. But perhaps it was *because* of that that she agreed to lying in bed with him. He looked wretched. Defenceless.

Alone.

Not for the first time she felt fury rising in her throat that Kilian had thought it prudent to tell her to leave him alone for days. But she was angrier at herself, for listening to him. Elina had been so excited by the prospect of creating a new overcoat for her stupid, immature king that she'd only too eagerly taken the reprieve from being by his side in order to work and work and work on the garment, hidden away in the servant's quarters until dark.

*I won't have a king to gift the damn thing to at this rate,* Elina thought as Kilian poked his pale head above the covers, still shocked that she'd agreed to lie in bed with him. But she could see him shivering - could *hear* his teeth chattering - and so she knew there was no way the man would warm up enough on his own. It also meant...

Elina's face flushed as she looked down at her clothes. She wouldn't be much use to Kilian as a body warmer if she kept them all on. With a sigh she began to unlace her dress, slipping it off as Kilian watched with wide, disbelieving eyes.

"Take that ragged overcoat off," she ordered without looking at him.

"You're being serious right now, aren't you?"

"Do you want to be warm or not?"

Kilian didn't respond, his silence being all the compliance Elina needed. He squirmed and struggled beneath the covers, whilst Elina wondered if she needed to remove her undershirt, too.

*Surely not,* she thought, but when she caught a glimpse of Kilian's expression - hungry despite the sickness that still lingered there - a brazen part of her lifted the shirt up and over her head before she could think better of it.

"Let down your hair, Elina."

It hadn't been the words she was expecting, in truth, now that she was standing naked in front of Kilian, the firelight casting her golden skin in a sunset glow. She fingered the braid wrapped around her head, somehow feeling far more nervous about letting down her hair than she was about being stark naked. But Kilian had practically seen her naked already – he hadn't seen her hair down. Apart from her mother nobody had.

Slowly, carefully, she unravelled the braid, working her fingers through her hair to loosen the curls until a cascade of wavy, tawny hair came tumbling down her back and over her shoulders. She glanced at Kilian from beneath her lashes, feeling somewhat uncertain, but that feeling was forgotten when she saw the way he was looking at her.

"You – you are so beautiful."

And though Daven had said the same thing, and though other people in Alder were beginning to make similar comments now, too, there was a world of difference in hearing them say Elina was beautiful and hearing *Kilian* say it.

*It shouldn't affect me so much,* she thought, though her cheeks were burning. *I already knew he liked the look of me. Him saying I'm beautiful isn't that important.*

Wordlessly Elina slid beneath the covers, heart hammering in her chest so loudly Kilian would definitely have heard it if the storm outside wasn't almost deafening. But when Kilian wrapped an arm around her waist and pulled her close she immediately recoiled.

"You're freezing!" she bit out. She'd never felt a human being so cold before. "And you're naked! I only told you to take your overcoat off."

Kilian snorted; Elina turned to face him, arms clutched protectively to her chest, though it was hardly as if either of them could see much in the dim light of the room, beneath the covers.

"Why should you be the only one naked?" he said.

"Hardly seems fair to me. And of course I'm freezing – I thought that was the point of you joining me. To warm me up."

"It...it is. But how could you possibly be so cold and still alive? Are you made of ice?"

His eyes were the colour of flint in the darkness, and at her comment they grew as hard as the stone, too. "Maybe I am. It would explain how heartless I am."

"You really are a pathetic excuse for a human being, Kilian."

He sighed, and some of the hardness in his eyes went away. "I know. What would you have me do? I *feel* pathetic. I feel wretched. I feel freezing."

With trepidation Elina reached a hand out and just barely touched Kilian's chest. She traced her fingers along his collarbone, brushing pale, tangled hair out of the way in the process. She took a deep breath, then wrapped her arms around the man's neck and pushed her body as close to his as she could possibly get it.

Kilian was so cold it physically hurt her to do so; Elina persisted anyway. She had to wonder if the curse had something to do with his abysmal core body temperature, and if that meant Kilian would be likely to run a constant fever once summer hit.

She nuzzled her head against his neck and mumbled, "Get warm and go to sleep," withholding a flinch when Kilian slid an arm around her waist and pressed his legs around one of hers.

"I'm fairly certain going to sleep isn't on my mind anymore..."

Elina glanced up; Kilian's expression was filthy. She noted with relief that his teeth were no longer chattering.

"This coming from the man who, thirty minutes ago, told me he couldn't keep any food down? I'd personally rather not do anything that involved you moving in the slightest, Kilian."

He bent his head down, brushing his lips against Elina's. "I needn't be the one doing the moving."

She dug her nails into his back. "Go to sleep!"

"Feel free to dig into me harder next time," Kilian smirked, but then he rested his chin on top of Elina's head and sighed contentedly. "I'll go to sleep. Thank you for this, Elina."

She didn't say anything; she wasn't used to hearing genuine gratitude fall from Kilian's tongue. Instead, she listened to the raging storm outside until it almost seemed to calm, but by the time she thought to look and see if it truly had she'd already fallen asleep.

*

When Elina woke she was facing away from Kilian, though he still held her close with an arm around her waist. It was very dark in the room – the fire had burned itself down to a smoulder. Outside the window it was almost silent. Almost. For it seemed as if, beneath the quiet, Elina could hear...something. Like the fall of snow on top of more snow, though she should never have been able to hear that, or the soft whistling of the wind winding through the forest, though she couldn't hear that either.

Elina was confused; why were her ears playing tricks on her? She wondered if it was simply because everything was so quiet where before there had been noise. It was discomforting. It set her on edge; caused her heart to pound.

It was then she realised Kilian was no longer freezing, nor was he hot from alcohol and steaming bathwater. He was merely...warm. Warm against Elina's back, warm against her legs, warm against...

*Oh.*

Kilian shifted behind her, just enough that she could feel a very telling hardness pressing against her thigh. It sent a heat flaring up her that had entirely nothing to do with being nestled beneath blankets against the cold. Elina desperately wanted to turn – to see if Kilian was awake or aware of his own body – but she didn't want to risk rousing him if he was fast asleep.

She moved slightly, trying to find a more comfortable way to sleep against Kilian that didn't send her mind racing. When his hand ended up moving from her waist to brush past her breasts Elina sucked in a breath.

*How can he be doing this fast asleep? How can he be driving me insane without even trying?*

But then Kilian's hand twitched, and he just barely squeezed one of her breasts before proceeding to stroke her skin. His other arm snaked around her, pressing Elina's hips against him until she cried out.

"You're awake, aren't you?" she bit out, heart beating so painfully she thought it might jump out of her chest. Elina blew some of her hair away from her face, staring at her hands and wondering what to do with them – what *Kilian* wanted her to do with them.

"Evidently," was all he said, and it sounded so reassuringly like sarcastic, cruel, drunk Kilian Hale that Elina almost turned around and slapped him. But she didn't, and Kilian took that as permission to proceed with his exploration. His hands went roaming, sliding, pinching and squeezing every available part of Elina's body until she was writhing beneath them.

"St-stop it, Kilian," she stammered. "You're not well. You need to –"

"Don't tell me I need to sleep. I know what I need." A pause, and then, "Turn around, Elina."

She shook her head, so nervous she didn't trust her voice. Kilian clucked his tongue, affronted, before bending his head slightly in order to kiss Elina's shoulder where it met her neck. When he began sucking on it she raised a hand to stop him, but Kilian grabbed it and sucked her fingers, instead.

When he rocked his hips against Elina's she let out a moan despite herself.

"Do you really not want to do this?" Kilian whispered against her ear, voice all water over gravel and shiver-inducing.

"I...I don't know what to do," Elina admitted, voice barely audible even though everything was quiet. "What am I supposed to do?"

"All you have to do is turn around."

She turned.

Kilian's mouth found hers immediately, a hand in her hair tilting her head to meet his. Deftly he shifted Elina until she was no longer beside him but beneath him. She was shocked by the weight of him, for though Kilian hadn't eaten in days and had been ravaged by fever he was, ultimately, still a man who towered over her when she stood beside him.

When Elina pulled away from the kiss to catch her

breath, Kilian watched her intently. His almost colourless eyes held the dying embers of the fire inside them. Along with his wild, tangled hair and sharp cheekbones he really did look like a man cursed.

*Or possessed,* Elina thought, as Kilian gently ran the back of his hand across her jawline with barely-contained desire. She could *feel* it on the air - the tightly-wound tension that he was dying to break. Longing to break. And she wanted it too. But she was frightened; how could she not be?

"I'll show you what to do," Kilian said, voice a low growl. "I won't hurt you. Just...stay here, beneath me, and help me chase the storm away."

"Well when you put it like that," Elina said, the edges of her lips quirking upwards despite herself, "then how could I possibly refuse my king?"

"Shut up," Kilian laughed, for just a second, and then Elina kissed him, and there were no more words spoken between them.

# Chapter Sixteen

***Kilian***

When Kilian woke he discovered several things. One: his head no longer felt like it was being split open with a white-hot axe. Two: he actually felt hungry, and instinctively knew that he'd be able to stomach whatever he next ate. Three: he wasn't cold. And, most importantly, four: he wasn't alone.

Elina lay in his arms, sleeping softly with her head against his chest. Her long, bronze hair was almost as wild and unruly as Kilian's was, which wasn't surprising considering what they had spent much of the night doing.

He glanced out the window and almost cried in shock.

The sky was clear. Not a single cloud broke up the pale, glorious blue of it. By the angle of the sun - the *sun*, which Kilian could see for the first time in months - he estimated that it had to be just past noon. He wished the sunlight slanting into the room would reach his bed, so it could reflect off Elina's hair and skin and allow Kilian to see her for the first time as what she truly was: a woman far too warm and exotic for Alder, and Kilian's castle, and Kilian himself.

And yet Elina *was* with him, in one capacity or another. All he wanted to do was while away the rest of the day watching her sleep, but as Kilian thought that she seemed to rouse, turning away from Kilian to land on her back. She yawned, stretching her arms above her head as she slowly opened her eyes, taking a few moments to blinks focus into them before locating Kilian by her side.

She smiled sleepily. "Morning, Your Royal –"

"I'm rather certain I told you to stop calling me that. Numerous times, in fact."

"Sorry; that doesn't ring a bell."

Kilian smoothed back Elina's hair, clearing it from her beautiful face. "Did you sleep well?"

"I suppose I did, though I could do with more."

"So go back to sleep."

Elina seemed to consider this for a moment but, upon realising how bright the room was, immediately sat up despite her nakedness. She stared out the window, wide-eyed; Kilian stared at her, instead.

"It isn't snowing."

"I know."

"Or stormy."

"I know."

"The sun is out."

"...I know."

She glanced at Kilian. "Did you hit your head or forget to be miserable or something?"

He pushed her back against the pillows in indignation and ran a hand through his matted hair that was in desperate need of a wash. "Are you telling me you want to get stuck in the castle once more? Because I'm sure I could make that happen."

Elina laughed softly. She touched Kilian's knee. "You're still warm. That's good."

"You're talking like you expected to wake up and find me dead. I'm not as fragile as all that."

"Could have had me fooled. How are you feeling in general? Any pain? Fever?"

Kilian cocked his head to the side when Elina reached up to press a dainty hand to his brow. "I feel... normal, I guess. I don't really know what normal is, though. But no pain. Or numbness. Just..."

"Normal," she smiled. "I know what you mean. Are you hungry? Want me to go and prepare –"

"Do you really think I'm expecting you to act as my servant after everything that's now happened between us?" Kilian asked, shaking his head incredulously. "I'll have a couple of servants prepare the dining room, and we can have a bath and take our time before having breakfast...or lunch, considering the time."

Elina quirked an eyebrow. "*We* can have a bath before having lunch together? A lot of presumptions there about my willingness to spend time with you."

"I thought *I* was the cruel one, Miss Brodeur," Kilian said, feigning hurt as he collapsed beside Elina, turning his head until their noses were almost touching. "Lately you've said far crueller things than I."

"You must be rubbing off on me."

Kilian said nothing; the look he gave Elina spoke volumes. Her face flushed a furious scarlet, but when she tried to look away Kilian slid a hand through her hair and pulled her back towards him. He kissed her, softly at first and then harder, harder, harder. By the time he was done Elina was gasping for breath.

His eyes glittered with desire as he watched her chest heave. "How are *you* feeling this morning, Elina?"

"As if...I spent the night in a man's bed for the first time."

"How apt. Do you care to spend another?"

Elina's brow creased uncertainly. "I really need to go home tonight. An afternoon, though..."

Kilian grinned foolishly, which for the first time was a good thing.

"That sounds good to me."

# Chapter Seventeen

***Elina***

"Elina. Elina...? *Elina*!"

Elina turned, surprised to see Scarlett Duke running through the glittering snow covering the forest path towards her. With the weather having been so glorious over the past three days they weren't the only people walking beneath the trees, basking in the scent of the winter sun beating down on dark pine needles.

She smiled bashfully. "Sorry, I was lost in thought."

"About something good, by the look on your face," Scarlett replied, linking her arm with Elina's as easily as if they were sisters. "Walk with me; keep me company whilst I stretch my legs."

Elina was only too happy to oblige. It was good for her to have a distraction, otherwise she'd end up daydreaming about Kilian once more. Not that daydreaming about him was a *bad* thing. Rather, it was a very good thing. It simply wasn't appropriate brain fodder during the daytime...especially not around other people.

"Sorry for not being able to speak with you when you were in the tavern the other day," Scarlett said, leading Elina out of the forest in full view of the castle. In the wintry light she could see that the smooth-stoned walls were not quite as grey as she'd first thought; there was a warm cast to the stone she hadn't noticed before. The warmth acted as a nice contrast to the slate blue roof tiles and delicate spires, which, during the multitude of stormy days Alder had been subject to so far, could barely be seen through the snow.

"That's alright," Elina replied, letting go of Scarlett's arm in order to hop forwards onto a stone-covered rock and slide back down to the path. "I was rather preoccupied, after all."

"Yes, it seems like the town has quite suddenly warmed to you," Scarlett said, a knowing smile on her face. "Particularly the man who was sitting next to you."

Elina's face flushed despite herself. "Daven. Yes, he's..."

"Oh, I see how it is. Something tells me you're not quite as interested in him as he is in you, though."

"I...yes. I suppose that's true. I haven't really thought much about it, to be honest."

"Because you've been thinking about someone else?"

Scarlett's eyes darted to the castle and back to Elina, who was mortified.

"I don't – it's nothing like –"

Scarlett merely laughed. "I don't mean to tease you. You're just...very obvious. You remind me of me a couple of winters ago."

"I somehow doubt that," Elina said as she glanced at the castle. She wondered if Kilian was looking out at his kingdom through a window, wishing he could enjoy the sunny day just like everyone else. It made her heart hurt.

Scarlett watched her every expression carefully. "I really was especially naive and transparent when I was eighteen. It's only because of Adrian's debatable influence that I've grown any kind of sense."

"Wait, you're only twenty?"

Scarlett nodded. "How old did you think I was?"

"I...don't know. Not the same age as I am. You're far more mature than me."

"Two years of travelling will do that to you. If you stay in one place for too long you cannot grow."

Elina rolled her eyes. "You sound like my mother."

"Then she's a wise woman."

"And yet she could have left Alder whenever she liked - even *with* me in tow - but she didn't. If you can't take your own advice then what use is it to someone else?"

Scarlett smiled wanly, brushing away a fine layer of snow from a boulder before perching on top of it. "Everybody has different circumstances. Have you ever asked your mother why she didn't leave once you had grown a little older?"

"No," Elina sighed, hating the admission. She really *did* sound naive and foolish compared to Scarlett. She dropped down to sit in the snow, not caring about her cloak and dress getting wet. "No, I never have. I always just assumed she'd give me an excuse, like not wanting to leave the shop or hoping things would get better for me with the children my age."

Scarlett chuckled. "Those sound like valid reasons, not excuses. Your priorities change when you have a child."

"You..." Elina stared at her doubtfully. "Do you have a child?"

"No, but I have two much younger brothers. And...a complicated family history. So I understand how your mother feels?"

Elina knew she shouldn't pry. She did anyway. "How complicated is complicated?"

"My father fell into bed with a local girl months before he was due to get married and she got pregnant, then left the child - me - on his doorstep. He raised me with my step-mother, though I didn't know she wasn't my birth mother until I was sixteen. Things got worse for a while after that. Much, much worse..." Scarlett stared up at the sky; her blue eyes were slightly too bright. "But then they got better. I'm very close with my step-mother now. In fact, I'd never even call her that. She *is* my mother, just as she always has been. You're crying, Elina."

It took Elina a few moments to process Scarlett's final sentence. When she did, she frantically rubbed her face with the heel of her hand until the tears were gone. "I'm sorry," she mumbled. "I can't believe I asked such an intrusive question. You didn't have to tell me all of that."

Scarlett merely smiled. "Your mother told me and Adrian about your father; I'm merely returning the favour, since you did not get a choice in whether we found out about your past or not."

Elina swallowed a lump in her throat that threatened more tears. A shiver ran down her spine as melted snow began to seep into her clothes. "Did you ever think about finding her? Your birth mother, I mean. Did your father tell you anything about her?"

"Yes and no. I wanted to know for so long - what did she look like, what was her family like, did my father know where she was - but when it came down to it I realised I didn't need to know. I started seriously asking myself what I would *do* if I found her. Ask her why she left me on my father's doorstep? That much was obvious; he was wealthy and she was not. He could raise me without any shame whereas a young mother with a child born out of wedlock would be scorned...but you know this very well already."

"Yes, rather well," Elina laughed bitterly. "Though I'm finding that it bothers me less and less with every passing day. The scorn, I mean. And being ignored. Being lonely."

"Is that because the townspeople are paying attention to you now?"

She shook her head. "No. That's...nice. It's gratifying, too, don't get me wrong. But it's hollow at the same time. They're only accepting me now that I've managed to do something *worthy* of their acceptance, even though I've been making their clothes for years and helping keep them warm."

"So what else changed?"

Elina glanced at the castle before she could stop herself and immediately regretted it.

"I *knew* you must have your eye on someone, but a

king? You have very high standards!" Scarlett grinned. Elina was tempted to throw a snowball at her.

"He isn't even the king, not truly," she grimaced. "He's the prince regent."

"Doesn't make a difference from where I'm standing. Does he know how you feel? Have you told him? What does he think about –"

"I think you're overwhelming Elina," came a low, melodic voice. Adrian approached them from the forest, dark red cloak starkly contrasting against the perfect snow. When he reached Scarlett, perched on her boulder, he kissed her gently.

Scarlett pouted. "I wasn't really. I just got excited."

Elina laughed nervously. "It's fine. And it's... complicated, I guess." She looked at the castle once more, thinking of Kilian trapped inside. "Can I trust the two of you?"

Adrian's reply was immediate. "Absolutely not."

Scarlett swatted his arm. "Don't be cruel. Is your mother not faring far better than she was before, Elina?"

Slowly, she nodded.

"And have I not just told you about my own past?"

She nodded once more.

Scarlett smiled. "Then I'd say you can trust us."

Elina said nothing for a few moments, still staring at the castle. When eventually she spoke her voice was soft and quiet. "He can't get out. Kilian – the prince regent, I mean – is stuck in the castle."

Adrian and Scarlett grew serious immediately. The man's eyes glittered with interest; leaning against the boulder Scarlett was sitting on he gestured for Elina to continue.

She sighed, then committed to telling them the rest. She wasn't sure at first if she could remember everything Kilian had said about his curse, given that she'd been drunk at the time, but as she spoke Elina realised she'd learned almost every word by heart. When she finished explaining Scarlett looked sad. Adrian's face was unreadable, his strange, amber eyes staring at the castle as if he might be able to see through the stone. Elina wondered if he actually could.

"That would explain the magic on you," he murmured, still looking at the castle. "Elina, did your royal friend happen to tell you anything about *how* the curse was said? For example, what his father was doing when he spoke the words, or whether they were spoken directly to his son or to an object?"

She shook her head. "Kilian told me he was in bed, and that his father must have thought he was asleep. All he heard were the words; I don't think even he knows more than that."

"Hmm."

Elina didn't know what else to say. She'd always thought that if she told Scarlett and Adrian about Kilian's curse that they'd be able to immediately help her. She hadn't thought about how complicated magic itself was at all.

She felt so foolish.

"Elina, can you get us some more information?" Scarlett asked.

Adrian nodded his assent. "Can you wander the castle and see if there's anything...unusual?"

She frowned. "Unusual how?"

"You'd know it if you saw or felt it, I think," Adrian said, which was infuriatingly vague. "Anything else you can get the king to remember would be helpful, too. And don't forget the servants. They might know something their sovereign doesn't."

Bleakly Elina thought about how Kilian had fired most of them. She wondered if she could find some of them in Alder, now that the townspeople were speaking to her.

So she nodded. "I'll see what I can find out."

"In the meantime..." Adrian glanced upward. "Perhaps try and keep the moody king in a pleasant frame of mind. I rather like the sun."

"Adrian!"

He smiled warmly for Scarlett. "You agree with me, though."

"Of course I do but you have no *tact.*"

"But it's obvious Elina must have had a hand in the king's better mood. Elina, I don't suppose you're currently bedding –"

"*Adrian*!"

Elina could only watch the pair of them enviously. Their relationship was so easy. So...free. She had never witnessed a pair like them before.

*They're certainly a far cry away from me and Kilian, who spend half our time at each other's throat and the other half of the time feeling miserable for ourselves.*

The thought gave Elina pause. Was she really thinking of herself and Kilian as a *couple?* Could they really be described as that? She didn't think so. For if

Kilian's curse was broken he'd run away as fast as was physically possible, regardless of whether Elina went with him or not. She wondered if he'd even want her to go with him.

*And would I want to go, either?*

But such thoughts were premature. Elina first had to focus on a solution to Kilian's curse. Freeing him from his prison wasn't going to be easy, after all. It might even be impossible, and he would be stuck in the castle for the rest of his life.

She didn't want to think about that.

# CHAPTER EIGHTEEN

***Kilian***

Kilian was lounging by the large, ornate windows in the dining hall. They offered an expansive view of the grounds to the back of the castle, including his beloved hot springs. He hadn't looked at them since he'd been forcibly handed the throne. He couldn't bear to.

But he was doing a lot of things he couldn't bear to do before, including being sober and treating what few servants he had at his disposal kindly, so Kilian figured he could handle looking down on the one part of his country that he actually liked.

And Elina was down below, exploring on uncertain feet, which was the primary reason Kilian was looking out of the window in the first place. He'd never admit that to anyone, though. He didn't even want to admit it to himself.

*I'm sickeningly soft with no alcohol in my blood,* he thought with a grimace. *Even my outward appearance is soft.* Kilian scratched his chin; it was clean-shaven and smooth. His long hair, which used to run past his shoulders in matted knots, was meticulously washed and combed and braided, keeping it away from his face.

His clothes were unstained and fresh; his ragged overcoat was nowhere in sight. The embroidered waistcoat he wore over his white shirt made Kilian feel oddly constrained, though he supposed that was a given considering he'd been living in shirts three sizes too big for him with ineffectual trousers and little else.

Though he would never say he was happy about it, he looked far more like a prince that he'd ever done before. Kilian could tell the servants felt the same way, though they were still nervously testing the air with their 'reborn' regent. It was reasonable of them to expect that Kilian would simply grab a bottle of vodka and revert to who he was two weeks before, after all, so he couldn't blame their shifty expressions and furtive footsteps.

*I need more staff,* he thought, tearing his eyes away from the window in order to look around the dining room. Kilian had wanted to eat in here with Elina after she'd spent the night in his bed; it hadn't happened. The room had been too filthy, with most everything in it covered in dust. It had since been cleaned to its former glory, but it was only one room out of dozens in the castle. He couldn't expect three servants to ever hope of keeping the place in check.

Kilian laughed derisively as he returned to watching Elina. His original intention of making the castle so filthy and neglected simply so Gabriel would have to deal with fixing it when he returned from war seemed so stupid now. Immature. Pointless.

Worst of all, it would have only proven to his brother just how useless he was. This wasn't something he'd ever cared about before - rather, he had thrived on disappointing him - but now things were different. Kilian had a clear head. He wasn't in pain. He could *think.* And though the cold was still there, seeping into Kilian's very soul and demanding he drink to forget about it, he could resist. If he fell prey to it then all he was doing was dying.

Kilian didn't want to die. He knew that now. All he wanted was to be free, and to do that he had to get his act together and work things out. For curses could be broken if he could only work out how.

*And she may be the key.* Kilian tracked Elina through the window with hawk-like eyes, observing her every movement. There didn't *seem* to be anything magical about her, but it wasn't as if magic was inherited like the colour of one's hair and eyes. But Elina was smart and could see right through Kilian. Most importantly, she hadn't abandoned him. She *wanted* to help him. And, though she might not yet be willing to admit it, Kilian knew that Elina liked him, even though he was an entirely unlikable person.

He had never wanted someone to like him before; having women be superficially attracted to him for a single night had always been enough. But Kilian wanted more for himself now. He wanted to *give* more to Elina.

"She's so beautiful," Kilian uttered, words fogging the window as he traced Elina with a finger against the freezing glass. The sun - which was more Elina's doing than Kilian ever wanted her to know - shone brightly in her hair, bringing out copper and gold and red tones usually hidden in the brown. Her skin was soaking up the sun like a sponge; it had already grown a shade or two darker in the week since the weather took a turn for the better. It made her look even more out of place against the snow.

Kilian longed to go somewhere together with her where snow didn't fall at all.

*When I'm free,* he thought longingly. *If that ever happens.*

It was dizzying to Kilian, how much he liked Elina. And he could never tell her. Or, rather, wouldn't. Despite everything that had happened so far - all of the ugly confessions, unruly behaviour and deadly storms - part of him was too prideful to admit how much the woman affected him.

*I want to fix myself by myself. I don't want to fall apart the second she's gone. I need to be better than that.*

For of course Elina could never be expected to leave with Kilian if that's what he ended up doing. Likewise, he couldn't demand that she stay either. Part of him itched to order her to do what he wanted simply because he could, but he buried that awful inclination away.

No. Elina deserved to decide what she wanted to do with her own life - to have free choice. How could Kilian deny her the one thing he was stripped of, after all?

A flash of movement outside brought Kilian out of his head. Elina was nowhere to be seen. For one agonisingly long second Kilian didn't know what to do or think, for at the end of the day if Elina had somehow been spirited away what *could* he do, stuck in the castle as he were?

But then Elina appeared - in the hot springs. She had fallen in, resurfacing from the water with a shocked and appalled expression on her face.

Kilian couldn't help it; he burst out laughing, the mirthful sound echoing around the dining hall and amplified ten times over. Elina couldn't hear him, of course, and she was unaware that she was being watched as she slipped and struggled out of the hot springs and onto the snow, shivering violently within seconds.

"Marielle!" he called out, knowing that the servant in question was probably nearby. Perhaps because she was the one he'd first shown kindness to, Marielle had in turn been the first of the castle's staff to warm to him. And now that Elina was far less Kilian's personal servant and more a willing companion, Marielle had stepped in to fill her shoes.

"Yes, sire?" she asked politely as she stepped foot into the dining hall.

"Prepare a bath in my room. I rather think somebody needs it."

Sneaking a glance through the window, Marielle's lips twitched when she spied Elina. She nodded her head at Kilian before retreating from the hall. Once Kilian could no longer see Elina through the window he, too, exited the hall, stalking purposefully down the main corridor. Knowing that Elina wouldn't be using the front doors but rather the servant's entrance, he took a few detours with quickening strides, hoping to reach the door before Elina entered the castle.

He made it just in time to catch her coming in, sodden, freezing and looking thoroughly ashamed of herself.

"Have a nice swim?" Kilian chided, his voice full of laughter he could barely suppress.

Elina's mouth widened into a shaky, wordless O at

the sight of him. His lips quirked upwards at the expression, then with no further comment he bodily lifted Elina over his shoulder and carried her away.

She cried out in surprise. “K-Kilian, what are you -”

“You’ve given me plenty of baths; it’s high time I gave you one.”

Elina had nothing to say in response, though Kilian felt her heart rate accelerate against his back as her hands clenched and unclenched his shirt.

A coiling down below his stomach told him the bath was unlikely to be a solo one.

# CHAPTER NINETEEN

***Elina***

"Kilian...?"

Elina spoke his name very softly, testing to see if the man was awake. But Kilian was fast asleep beside her, snoring quietly as he rolled onto his back. In the moonlight he was so pale Elina thought he looked more a statue than a living thing. Only the gentle rise and fall of his chest belied the fact that Kilian was a mortal, breathing man.

Kilian was looking much better now that he'd gotten over his alcohol withdrawal. His appetite had voraciously returned, too, and he'd started taking much better care of his appearance. Though he'd been handsome in his wild, unkempt state, now that Kilian was groomed and fed Elina came to the conclusion that he was undeniably beautiful.

With a tentative finger she prodded his cheek. Nothing. Kilian didn't even stir. And so Elina slowly crept out of bed, locating her undershirt on the floor before realising that she'd definitely wake the sleeping prince if she tried to lace on her dress.

She glanced at the door leading to Kilian's cavernous selection of clothes that he rarely touched. Slipping on her undershirt, Elina tiptoed over and perused through his trousers with only the light from the moon to guide her eyes. Eventually she came across a dark pair that seemed as if they were far too short for Kilian – likely a relic from his younger days. As quietly as possible she pulled them on, somewhat impressed that they fit reasonably well if she ignored how tight they were around her hips.

Elina knew where the creaky floorboards were in Kilian's chambers by now, so it wasn't difficult to largely avoid them in order to sneak out to the corridor. She teased tangles out of her hair with her fingers and braided her hair down her back as she walked, alternately peering then shying away as she passed through shadow, then moonlight, then shadow as a result of the tall, narrow windows that punctuated the walls.

Now that she had left Kilian's room Elina had to admit that she really didn't know what she was looking for, surrounded by swathes of empty, cold, magic-ridden castle walls.

*It's hardly as if Adrian and Scarlett were helpful on that front. They were so vague! How am I supposed to* know *what I'm looking for when I see it? It's not as if I'm well-versed in magic myself.*

Real magic – true, powerful curses and spells – was so rare these days. Elina knew from the books she'd read growing up that some countries didn't believe it existed at all. For a while in her youth she had entertained this idea, simply because she wanted to hate her so-called magician father rather than long to meet him.

Elina had no such naivety to fall back on now. She knew magic was real. The dangerous kind.

She had to work out what was going on.

Though Elina had spent almost a month in the Hale family castle she was still unfamiliar with much of it. Kilian had only recently wanted the place cleaned up after months of allowing it to go to ruin, so aside from his own chambers, the servants quarters, throne room and dining hall Elina didn't know what much else of the castle was actually used for.

She climbed down the grand staircase first; the dining hall was at the bottom, with a sprawling ballroom attached on its left. Vaguely recalling that Kilian once told her there was a library to the right of the hall, she tentatively pushed on what was hopefully a promising door.

Peering through the darkness, and treading on feet made silent from a layer of dust, Elina realised very quickly that the room wasn't a library so much as a parlour room which happened to contain a few bookshelves.

*I suppose Kilian would consider that a library,* she mused, using what little light was available to try and discern the titles of the heavy tomes closest to her. *He doesn't seem like much of a reader.*

Many of the books were handsomely-bound encyclopaedias and atlases. A few were record books, full of lists of farm stocks, taxes, town names and various other things Kilian definitely needed to know about but deliberately hadn't bothered learning.

But nothing stood out. If Adrian was sure Elina

would *know* what she was looking for when she saw it then it definitely wasn't in the parlour. Exiting, she briefly tried the dining room, which she already knew likely held nothing of interest. She paused in front of several portraits of the royal family through the years, smothering a laugh when she came across one in which a scowling, huffing boy of around four seemed to try his best to ruin the portrait.

*That must be Kilian,* she thought, sparing a look at his older brother Gabriel, who looked every inch the perfect prince. *My mother thought so, too, but if he really was 'perfect' then why has he still sent no word back to Kilian about why he's delayed at the border?*

Shaking her head, Elina left the room and headed back up the grand staircase, and then up a further set of stairs that headed in a westward direction. The entire wing of the castle she entered was grandly decorated; it didn't take her long to realise that she must be in the *actual* king's chambers. It was only in realising this that Elina acknowledged that Kilian's chambers were, indeed, his own rooms. He'd probably lived in them from infancy.

*He doesn't strike me as the kind of person who'd take over his parents' room, even if it* was *the king's bedroom,* she mused. When she reached a highly polished, heavy set of wooden doors Elina felt her heart beat quicken. An overwhelming desire to run back downstairs to Kilian's bed without continuing her search hit her, but upon noticing that one of the doors was ajar her curiosity overtook that desire.

The door swung silently outward despite its weight. Inspecting the lushly carpeted floor Elina noticed that there were footsteps through the dust, leading to a desk the size of Elina's own bedroom back at her mother's house.

She walked towards it, careful to tread only in the footprints already embedded in the dust. On top of the dark, gnarled grain of the table sat a silver locket, shining in a narrow ray of moonlight that had wormed its way between the heavy, velvet curtains covering a full wall of the room.

Elina agonised over whether to touch it. But, just as when she couldn't help asking Scarlett about her complicated family history, Elina's reluctance quickly burned away in the face of something new and interesting. She picked up the locket, appreciating how the silver was etched with a complicated, beautiful pattern of vines and flowers on both sides.

When she pried it open a lock of silvery-blonde hair fell to the floor. Panicking, Elina only just managed to grab it before it brushed against the dust, securely replacing it back inside the locket and flinging the piece of jewellery onto the table before running out of the king's chambers without so much as another glance around.

*I don't care what Adrian said,* she thought as she fled down the stairs, *I have no idea what to look for. Even if I combed the castle a hundred times I'd come up blank.*

When she reached the bottom of the grand staircase Elina became aware that her hair had come undone from its braid. She shook it out and, in the process, saw the door to the ballroom out of the corner of her eye. She'd never been in before. It had only recently been cleared of dust, and Elina knew she'd be lying if she said she didn't want to look inside. So she walked over as quickly as she dared and opened the door, taking a moment to adjust to the relative blinding brightness of the room over the corridor.

Much of the southern wall of the ballroom was made of gilded-framed glass, providing a full view over the castle grounds and the mountain on which it was nestled into. The windows let in an overwhelming amount of moonlight, casting the enormous room in silvery, ethereal light. It was freezing, but that somehow added to the magical feel of the room. But the feeling was magical in the poetic sense; Elina sensed nothing awry about the place.

Taking a deep breath – though she wasn't sure why she was nervous – Elina entered the room, bare feet echoing on the polished floor. For a few moments she imagined herself dressed up to dance, instead of in an insubstantial white shirt and a royal prince's old trousers. She twirled and leapt across the length of the room, reassured by the quickness of her feet and her sense of balance. It had been too long since Elina hadn't been wrapped in restrictive winter clothes.

*Spring can't come quickly enough,* Elina thought. This time, however, the thought had nothing to do with leaving Alder alongside her mother. No, it had to do with spring feasts and summer dances and swimming in the mountain lakes and forcing Kilian along to experience all of these things with her – things she had previously experienced alone or not at all.

Elina knew she had to get back to bed. She'd been away too long and Kilian was sure to notice her absence soon. But the feeling of *space* around her – a space with nobody in it but her and the moon – was intoxicating. It was somehow the closest thing to freedom she had ever felt.

"Dancing by yourself seems awfully lonely."

Elina stopped so abruptly at the voice that she tripped over her feet. For there, by the doorway, stood Kilian, yawning good-naturedly and looking ridiculous in his ragged overcoat. It made her think of the one she was making him - the one that was mere days away from completion.

She almost grinned, but something about the way Kilian was looking at her now that he'd finished yawning stopped her. "I didn't mean to wake you," she said quietly, her voice reverberating off the walls turning it to a shout.

Kilian flicked his eyes downward. "Are those my trousers?"

"Possibly. Want them back?"

"No; they look good on you," he replied, shaking his head slightly. Kilian's hair caught the moonlight, turning it to silver. Elina had never once cared for the way the blonde hair of Alder looked beneath the sun and the moon before, but it was different with Kilian.

*Everything* was different with Kilian.

"Why are you in here, anyway?" he continued, walking towards Elina whilst flinching at the freezing temperature of the floor.

"I...couldn't sleep."

"You should have woken me up."

"You were too peaceful to wake up."

Kilian barked out a laugh as if the notion of him being peaceful was too incredulous to believe. When he reached Elina he bowed deeply, though it seemed more a mockery of a bow rather than a sincere one, especially considering his wretched clothes and slept-on hair.

Elina eyed him warily. "What are you doing, Kilian?"

"About to ask you to dance, of course," he replied, eyes glinting in the moonlight like ice as he held out a hand. "Though I must admit to being rather bad at it, given that I tend to avoid any and all social events befitting my station."

Elina slid a tentative hand into his; a shiver ran up her spine when he snaked his other hand around her back, beneath her shirt. "I thought you *enjoyed* such events so you could get drunk and disappoint your family?"

Kilian laughed harder at that. Pulling Elina closer to him, he took a step back and then another when she followed. Clumsily he spun her beneath his arm. "The point being that I was drunk instead of dancing, or too busy falling into bed with a -"

"I get it," Elina cut in, rolling her eyes. A few steps later and Kilian seemed to have found some kind of rhythm to follow and, a few steps after that, Elina almost felt as if they were beginning to glide across the floor. She frowned. "I thought you said you were bad at this?"

"I am, comparatively. My brother's outstanding at it; my parents were even better. But I guess the lessons they forced me to attend as a child haven't been entirely obliterated by my alcohol consumption throughout the years."

"You are so spoiled."

"I know."

When Elina reached up and kissed him Kilian looked somewhat surprised. But then he ran a hand up through her hair, crushing her lips back against his with an intensity that stopped their dancing altogether.

"What were you really doing, wandering the castle in the middle of the night?" he asked, voice a low, unsteady growl that told Elina it would be a long time before either of them fell back asleep once they returned to Kilian's bed.

She smiled slightly. "Looking for magic."

"Did you find any?"

"No." Elina pulled Kilian towards the door by his hand, interlacing her fingers through his. "Only you."

# Chapter Twenty

***Kilian***

Kilian was spending more and more of his time sat by various windows in the castle, watching the world go by whilst he was locked up inside. Especially when Elina returned to her mother's house, though at his insistence those occurrences had grown less and less frequent. He knew he should feel bad for taking up all of her time.

He didn't.

Kilian simply didn't have it in him to feel guilty about tearing Elina away from her mother and the town that now loved her in order to satisfy his own desires to be with her. Drunk or not, that part of him would never change. He felt good when he was with Elina. Useful. Motivated. Wanted. And he knew Elina enjoyed spending time with him too, so at the end of the day Kilian reasoned his selfishness wasn't hurting anyone.

But then he thought of Elina's mother, Lily, who Kilian had to constantly remind himself had been ill. She'd been the primary reason Elina had accepted his original deal; considering how unfairly he'd treated Elina back then she clearly had to love her mother very much to put up with him in exchange for her health.

*I suppose I can't expect everyone to have an unhealthy relationship with their parents, like me.*

Not for the first time in recent weeks Kilian thought of his own mother. He'd never had a bad relationship with her, so to speak, but because she'd been so sickly after giving birth to Kilian and largely committed to bed rest for her health he had hated her. She'd always been too unwell to spend time with him. The looks his father gave him were even worse, too; they told Kilian all he needed to know, even as a child.

Kilian's father blamed him for his wife's deterioration. It was unbearable. It was almost a relief when his mother died shortly after his sixth birthday, though in truth Kilian had grieved in secret, when nobody was watching. Always in secret.

He supposed that habit had carried on throughout his life – to acknowledge feelings only when alone.

*Because I was lonely.*

That was what he'd screamed at Elina, the moment he finally started to let her in even though he hadn't wanted to. She could have retreated. Could have run away. Instead, she stayed, and now Kilian couldn't imagine coping through a single day within the castle without her.

"I need to do something for her mother," he decided aloud, thinking about perhaps insisting a little stronger that Elina bring her up to stay in the castle. That way she could spend more time with her mother without Kilian having to sacrifice his own time with her.

He laughed derisively at how poorly-functioning a human being he was. *Lily Brodeur has her shop. That was one of the reasons Elina never wanted to move her to the castle. Who am I to ask the woman to give up her family's business simply for my benefit?*

Kilian's heart lightened immediately when he spied Elina making her way across the snow towards the castle. She was struggling with a large box in her arms; curious, he spared a few seconds to check his appearance in a mirror - something he'd never have done for anyone before - then lounged back on his bed as if he hadn't been impatiently watching and waiting from the moment he opened his eyes that morning for Elina to arrive.

His heart was thumping painfully in his chest. It wasn't like Kilian to be nervous, but ever since his and Elina's midnight dance in the ballroom it constantly felt as if he had something lodged in his throat. It was uncomfortable and suffocating.

Part of him knew that what was 'stuck' in his throat were all the words he wanted to say to Elina but never could. And yet there was something else, too; an uncertainty about what Elina had actually been doing, wandering the castle in the dead of night when he was asleep.

*She said she was looking for magic. But what? And why? Or...for whom?*

If she had been wanting to help Kilian then Elina would have asked him to help in her search. He knew the castle far better than she did, after all.

When Elina came through the door and smiled at Kilian strewn out on his bed all suspicions were forgotten. He didn't want to dwell on such things, especially when he was already obsessing over what his brother was up to. The servant Kilian sent down to the border was yet to return, even though he was two weeks late.

*It would definitely have taken him longer than four days as a round trip, so I was being unreasonable with my time frame, but even still...*

He shook the thought from his head. "What's in the box?" he asked Elina curiously when she placed it onto the bed beside him. "Secrets? Magic?"

Elina laughed softly. "No. Nothing like that. It's...a gift."

"For me?"

"No, for me. Of course for you, Kilian."

The look of tolerance on Elina's face at his stupid question filled him with unbearable affection for her. The lump in his throat returned; Kilian gulped it down. "Can I open it now?"

"Unless you want to lie there and stare at a box all day whilst I stand and watch you watching it."

He smirked. "Point taken."

But when Kilian sat up and reached out to take the lid off the box Elina grabbed his hand, her expression anxious and somewhat embarrassed.

"I'm - I'm still nowhere near as good as my mother is but I did try really hard with this and I hope you like it and -"

"Shut up, Elina."

Kilian took her hand away, altogether more interested in the gift now he knew Elina had made it herself. When he lifted the lid of the box she stood there, nervously biting her lip as if she were silently pleading for Kilian to like whatever was inside.

She needn't have worried, for when Kilian unfolded the long, high-collared, elaborately embroidered overcoat from the box he was instantly enamoured. The fabric was a dark, moody blue dashed through with silver thread that shone like gold in the light from the fire – like his hair. The interior fabric was soft and luxurious against his fingertips, promising to insulate him against the cold when he wore it. The buttons were engraved with a pattern of vines and flowers that seemed oddly familiar, though Kilian couldn't place it.

When Kilian didn't speak or react Elina only grew more worried. "Do you –"

"I love it. This is – why did you make this for me? *When* did you start making this? It must have taken weeks."

She blushed. "Just under three. I didn't do much else other than make it whenever I wasn't with you. I... decided to make it after we got drunk together. I couldn't stand watching you wear that ridiculous, moth-eaten overcoat of yours, and then the colour scheme and embroidery pattern came to me so quickly it almost felt like I had no choice but to make it."

Kilian was torn between trying on the garment and pulling Elina down onto the bed with him, to demonstrate his gratitude the only way he knew how – physically. But then he thought of the lump in his throat, and how his life would be so much better if it simply disappeared.

"Elina," he began, avoiding her eyes at first through sheer nerves. "I don't know how to thank you. For everything."

"You don't have to thank me, Kilian. I didn't do any of his for your gratitude."

"The fact you did anything at all for *me* means you get it regardless," he quipped. Gently placing the overcoat on top of its box Kilian got to his feet, gesturing for Elina's hand. When she gave him it he enveloped it in both of his; her skin was hot against his own. "I had no idea just how much I would come to depend on you when you first started working for me. You've completely changed me."

Elina wrinkled her nose. "I don't really think I've changed you, Kilian. You just didn't know who you were. And you're still insufferable and lazy, even though you've definitely gotten far more tolerable since you sobered up –"

"You really know how to ruin a moment, don't you?" Kilian laughed, shaking his head incredulously. When he locked eyes with her he realised how stupid it had been to pretend his feelings for her were trivial.

There were anything but.

"Elina –"

"Sire?"

Kilian and Elina frowned at each other, then simultaneously looked at the door. For there was the servant Kilian had sent to find out why his brother was delayed, looking uncertain and confused by the scene he had walked in on.

Kilian let go of Elina's hand immediately and stalked over to the man. "What have you found out?" he demanded, now on edge and nervous for an entirely different reason than confessing to Elina. Outside the wind violently buffeted the window, as sure a sign as any that Kilian had little to no control over his own feelings once they were forced to the surface.

"Your Royal Highness, he..."

"He's what?"

"He's..." The servant looked at the floor. "Missing, sire. Your brother is missing. He has been since that first messenger was sent."

Kilian roared in fury, the sound all but drowned out by the rapidly-forming storm outside. He turned from the servant, fervently pacing his room as the reality of what Gabriel being missing meant.

*It means he isn't coming back. It means I'm stuck here. It means I must be king.*

"Get out," he muttered to the servant. The man was only too happy to oblige, scurrying out of sight just as Elina reached his side and touched his arm.

"Kilian, there's a solution to all of this. You just have to stay calm and –"

"What do *you* know?!" he screamed, wrenching his arm away from Elina's hand as if she had burned him. She stared at him in shock.

"Kilian –"

"No, don't talk to me in that tone. You have *no idea* what's going on in my head right now."

"You have to find out if your brother is still alive!"

"Who cares about that? Dead or alive, he's gone, leaving me here to rot –"

"He's your brother!"

"*I don't care*!"

"Then you're an even worse liar than you think!" Elina screamed back at him. Kilian was momentarily taken aback – he'd never heard Elina raise her voice like this before. "There's no way you don't care for him," she continued on passionately, "he's all the family you have left."

Kilian averted his eyes. "Just because family matters to you doesn't mean it has to matter to me. I'm the one whose *father* cursed him to stay a prisoner forever."

"At least you had a father! And he clearly cared for you, whether you believe that or not. Have you never wondered what his true reasons were for placing you on the –"

"You know *nothing,* Elina. Nothing at all."

She glared at him. "If you would just *tell* me then I would."

"I don't owe you that. I don't owe anyone anything."

"I wouldn't want you to tell me because you feel like you owe me!" she cried, attempting for a second time to touch Kilian's arm. He shrugged her off. "I want you to tell me because you...want to tell me. Because you –"

"Just get out, Elina."

She blinked in surprise. "What?"

"Get out. Now."

Elina glanced out the window at the howling, wretched blizzard obscuring the sky. It seemed like a distant dream that the sun had ever been visible. "Kilian, don't –"

"Now!" he ordered, voice like thunder to match the storm. "Don't come back."

For a moment it seemed like Elina would protest.

There were tears streaming down her face; Kilian fought back the urge to wipe them away and apologise – to beg her to stay. But then she set her mouth in a grim line, pulled up the hood of her cloak and swiftly departed Kilian's chambers without another word. It was only when the echoing of Elina's footsteps were silenced that Kilian collapsed onto his bed and buried his face in the heartbreakingly beautiful overcoat she'd slaved away to make him.

*It's better this way,* Kilian thought, hating himself, but hating Gabriel more. *I should never have gotten close to Elina in the first place. I should have stayed alone, just like I have been from the very beginning. I could never have expected her to stay with me if I'm locked in this castle forever.*

If he had never let Elina in then turning her away would not have hurt quite so much.

Kilian had never been in so much pain.

# Chapter Twenty-One

*Elina*

"And here was me thinking we'd already had the worst of the winter weather."

"This is the ugliest storm to hit Alder for years."

"Even worse than when the magician –"

"Definitely worse than when the magician stepped in."

Most everyone in Gill's tavern glanced at Elina, then, though it wasn't out of spite or annoyance. Because of her they had enough supplies to make it through the awful winter, even with this new barrage of snow and hail and thunder. She doubted she'd ever be spurned by the town again. But she was still the daughter of the magician, so of course whenever he was brought up they thought of her.

"You'd think, after twenty-one years, they'd have something better to talk about," Lily sighed. Now that Elina had been accepted by the town, her mother had decided to venture out with her to enjoy the warmth and atmosphere of the tavern. Elina knew it was a thinly-veiled excuse to keep watch on her – she hadn't exactly returned from Kilian's castle in the best state of mind the previous day, after all.

Elina's only response to both her feelings and her mother's comment was to tip back the rest of the contents of her tankard of ale down her throat. She didn't know what else to do. She felt useless. Kilian had been beside himself with fury; Elina didn't think she'd ever seen a person so angry. But it wasn't simply that Kilian was *angry*. No, in the moments after learning that his brother was missing he'd had the expression of a doomed man, his life having been forcibly ended before it had ever really begun.

She sighed. Kilian's reaction wasn't even over-dramatic. In reality anyone would react the way he had if they were being forced to stay trapped inside the same building forever performing a role they never wanted. But what Elina didn't understand was Kilian's lack of concern about his brother's wellbeing.

*It's impossible that he doesn't care for Gabriel,* she thought, though in reality Elina could not be sure of this, given Kilian's personality. But the mere fact that, before they'd been interrupted, Kilian had clearly been planning to tell Elina something important – something about his feelings for her – suggested Kilian was not quite as heartless and callous as he pretended to be.

But Elina could do nothing to help him, not just because he had sent her away but because Elina had no idea how to help him. Kilian had been right; what *could* Elina do?

*Nothing, except stay by his side and support him.*

*But he doesn't want that.*

Sadly she thought of the way Kilian's face lit up when he saw the overcoat Elina had made him. She wished she could go back to that moment and stay in it, when curses and storms and thrones had been the last things on either of their minds.

"Elina? What's wrong?"

She shook her head, a small, humourless smile on her face. "Nothing, mama. I'm just...I don't know. Stuck."

Lily frowned at her daughter. "Stuck? How so? Has Daven –"

"It's nothing to do with Daven," Elina said quickly. In truth she hadn't thought about Daven since she first slept with Kilian. For her mother to bring him up now felt bizarre and out-of-place. It made Elina realise that she really had outgrown Alder and its people, even if they were welcoming to her now.

"So his brother really isn't missing?"

"You really think he could go *missing*? No, he ran off, I'm telling you."

Elina's ears pricked up at the conversation the group of men were having behind her. Noticing the change in her expression, Lily didn't try to continue their conversation. Instead she listened carefully alongside her daughter.

"How would you know that?" Fred, the town head, demanded. Clearly he didn't believe the other man.

"I was the one sent back to the castle to tell Prince Kilian that his brother was going to be delayed for a few weeks. It was all a ruse to buy Gabriel some time."

"But why would he do such a thing? To run off when there's a war going –"

"The war's done," the man interrupted. "As soon as Prince Kilian spoke to the foreign diplomats everything was tied up and sorted."

*Kilian doesn't know that,* Elina thought. It felt like her heart was simultaneously frozen and beating far too quickly.

Frederick clucked his tongue. "What in the world is going on? How as a country are we supposed to deal with a king who keeps our armies down at the border just so he can use them as a ruse to *run off*? And for what purpose?"

"A woman. It's always a woman."

"Why not bring the woman back with him and take his place on the throne?"

"Do you really think anyone in their right mind wants to live in a country where the winters are like *this*?" the man asked. Elina didn't need to see him to know that he was gesturing out the window towards the storm. "She's not from around here; she's from much further south, apparently."

"But living in a castle, married to a king...who wouldn't want that?"

Elina stood up abruptly, surprising everyone in the near vicinity. Her mother grabbed her arm.

"Where are you going, Elina? If you want to head home –"

"The castle," she muttered. The men who were talking stared at her, confused and unsure about what was going on. "Kil – the prince regent needs to know what's going on."

The messenger who'd been sent to tell Kilian of his brother's delay grew pale. "You cannot tell him. It was his brother's orders to keep him in the dark."

Elina rounded on him. "Tell me, who sits on the throne? And who has run off? You should have told the truth from the beginning. You have no idea what you've done."

"What I've - what have I done?!"

But Elina stormed out of the tavern before the man had finished his sentence, though her mother was shouting for her to return. She was furious. She was heartbroken.

*I scorned Kilian for not caring about his brother when clearly his brother does not care for him.*

Tears began to well up in Elina's eyes, burning painfully when the bitter wind blew against them. It really was too cold and tumultuous and dangerous to be outside. But if the weather was the way it was then Kilian himself could only be worse. Elina needed to see him. Talk to him. He needed to know what his brother had done.

When she finally reached the castle Elina could not feel her hands nor feet nor face. She was beyond freezing; even so, she struggled to the servant's entrance to the castle and banged upon the surface. But the door was locked, and after a few minutes Elina had to conclude that nobody was going to let her in.

Staggering through the snow drifts she made her way to the monstrously large front doors of the castle, once more pounding her numb, ice-cold fists against the wood and iron.

“Kilian, let me in!” she screamed. The wind carried her voice away as if it were nothing more than a whisper. She hit the door again. “Let me in! Let me in! Let me in! Kilian, I need to talk to you!”

But there was no response. Elina couldn’t even see well enough through the snow to know if Kilian was watching her from a window. And so she continued to bang against the door and shout until her throat was raw and her voice was hoarse, even though it was futile.

Eventually she could keep it up no longer. The cold began to make Elina tired – dangerously tired – so she leaned against the door. A few minutes later she slid down to the snow, her legs having lost the strength to keep her upright.

“Kilian,” she cried, her voice barely audible even to her. “I’m cold.”

He didn’t answer.

# Chapter Twenty-Two

***Kilian***

Kilian had been staring at a bottle of vodka for hours now. Every time he picked up the bottle, opened the lid and placed it to his lips something stopped him, which only made him more furious.

*I want to drink,* he thought. *I want to forget everything.*

He knew it was impossible.

Now that he was in full control of his senses he didn't want to willingly take them away. Kilian needed to work out a way to free himself of the curse placed upon him by his father, and for that he needed his brain to be fully functioning. But he couldn't work out *what* to do, or how. He didn't have access to a magician or even books on curses and spells to work from. Not for the first time, Kilian regretted how little he'd paid attention to the education his parents had so desperately tried to force upon him.

When the window rattled in its frame Kilian

jumped; it sounded dangerously close to shattering. With a sigh he dragged himself over to make sure the latch was securely in place, wincing at the noise the wind and hailstones made against the glass. He could see nothing outside but darkness and swirling, never-ending snow. With a sadistic grin Kilian thought of the town of Alder, the people fearfully huddled in their houses and clinging to the hope that the storm would soon pass.

*It won't,* he thought. *I'll make sure of that.*

He knew it wasn't fair, to punish other people for something his brother had done to him, but even if Kilian wanted to he wouldn't have been able to stop the freezing blizzard. He was too unstable; too furious; too lost.

When a tentative knock on the door drew Kilian's attention away from the window, he pulled his old, ragged overcoat a little closer against his chest and called the person in. He couldn't bear to look at the one Elina made him after how he'd treated her, much less wear it.

Marielle took a few steps into Kilian's chambers. "Your Royal Highness, please pardon the intrusion."

"That depends on what the intrusion is for," he replied, rubbing his temple to try and force a nagging headache away. Kilian didn't want to have to deal with people right now if he could at all avoid it.

"Miss Brodeur was attempting to enter the castle through the servant's door. We didn't let her in."

"Good."

Marielle glanced at Kilian uncertainly before casting her gaze to the floor. "She moved to the main entrance. I don't think she's left yet."

That gave Kilian pause. *What's she thinking,*

*travelling to the castle when the weather is so bad? She's a fool.*

"She'll get the message and return home soon enough," he said, hoping it to be true. "She's not stupid."

"It doesn't seem like she –"

"Thank you for letting me know, Marielle. You may go."

Kilian rushed back over to his window but, as before, he could see nothing but darkness and snow. Straining against the roar of the wind he tried to hear Elina shouting, but of course he couldn't. With any luck she'd already given up and gone home.

*I can't see her,* he thought. *I just can't. Not after what I said. And if I am to be trapped here forever then I don't want her feeling obligated to stay in Alder for my sake. She should just leave and forget about me.*

Such a thought hurt Kilian, ripping at his heart more than the cold ever could; he didn't *want* Elina to forget about him. But the chances of him being able to break his curse were so low. It wasn't something Elina should have to bear.

"Go home, Elina," he muttered into the darkness, before retreating to his bed and collapsing on top of it.

Kilian lay there for a while, staring up at his ceiling with sightless eyes in the hopes that eventually he would fall asleep.

He didn't.

After an hour or two he swung back up to his feet with the intention of wandering down to the kitchen to grab some food, though he wasn't hungry. But he had nothing else to do, and nothing new to think about.

Loneliness felt so much worse after knowing what it felt like to *not* be lonely.

A nagging impulse pushed Kilian to stop by the front doors first. They were heavy, and there was nobody around to help him open them, so he was reluctant to even try. But even so...with a whistle of breath through his teeth Kilian struggled to open one of the doors just wide enough for him to peer outside. At first he saw nothing out of the ordinary. No people. No shouting.

Kilian felt a wave of relief wash over him, though it was mixed with a keening sense of regret that he hadn't simply let Elina into the castle in the first place. And then –

A snow-covered figure fell through the gap in the door, a glimpse of blue material and dark hair only just visible beneath the ice that was dislodged when the person hit the floor with a thud.

"*No,*" Kilian mouthed, horrified beyond words. With shaking hands he dragged Elina inside and slammed the door behind them, holding her close to his chest as he stood and ran for help.

"Marielle!" he screamed. "Somebody! Anybody! Help me!"

Kilian could hardly bear to look at Elina's face as he ran for his room. She was unconscious; he couldn't even tell if she was breathing. And she was *pale,* a word Kilian would never have used to describe Elina's complexion before. She was colder than any living thing had a right to be.

When he reached his bed he gently placed Elina down upon it and removed her stiff, frozen cape and placed his head to her chest, checking for a heartbeat. It was just barely there.

"Run a bath!" he ordered a shocked Marielle when she appeared at the door. "Not too hot," he added on, remembering what his mother used to tell him about people who had been out in the cold for too long.

Kilian unlaced Elina's dress, silently apologising for doing something so shameful when she wasn't conscious. But he had to; he had to remove every last piece of snow-covered, sodden clothing that she had on. When she was naked Kilian held her in his arms and lay beneath the covers, smoothing snow out of her hair as he anxiously watched her blue lips, wishing they'd hurry up and return to their usual, irresistible colour.

"You idiot," he muttered through chattering teeth, "you obstinate idiot." Elina was so cold she almost burned his skin. Belatedly he wondered if this was what she'd felt like when Kilian had asked her to keep *him* warm in bed two weeks ago.

*No, this must be worse. I don't see how I was ever this cold.*

"S-sire, the bath is ready."

"Tend to the fire," he ordered, "then head to the kitchens and have some food prepared. Soup. Tea. Anything easy on the stomach." A few minutes later Marielle vacated his room, then Kilian lifted Elina out of bed and gingerly placed her in the bath. Marielle had done her job properly; the bath was a gentle temperature. The now roaring fire seemed to be competing with the wind outside in an effort to make as much noise as possible.

Kilian desperately wanted the fire to win.

Finding a cloth, he soaked the material and gently scrubbed Elina's face and washed her hair. "Come on, idiot," he begged her unconscious face, watching as her cheeks slowly began to regain some colour. "Wake up. You have to wake up."

It took a while before Elina's body finally seemed to return to an almost normal temperature, but she still didn't rouse when Kilian took her out of the bath, dried her off and dressed her in the large, luxurious robe she'd worn before, after the two of them had drunkenly taken a bath together. Then he sat her against his chest in front of the fire, feeling her heartbeat gradually speed up against his hand.

Marielle had been and gone with the food Kilian had requested before Elina finally, tortuously, began to wake. Her dark lashes fluttered, and a low moan escaped her lips.

"Elina!" Kilian cried out, turning her around to face him. "What were you thinking?! Have you lost your senses completely? What's *wrong* with you?"

"Kilian...?" Elina slurred, her brain struggling to work out where and when she was. But after a few blinks she finally seemed to properly wake up, and she tensed in Kilian's arms. Her eyes went wide. "Kilian - your brother -"

"You think I care about my brother right now?!" He crushed her against his chest, burying his face into her damp hair as he willed himself not to cry. "You almost died and you want to talk about my *brother*?"

But Elina feebly pushed him away with what little strength she had. "Kilian, you have to listen to me, please! You really think I sat in that storm just to tell you off again?"

Kilian was pained. He didn't want to talk about anything else that wasn't to do with himself and Elina. The rest of the world could burn - or freeze - for all he cared. Just so long as Elina was okay. But if she had really, stupidly risked her life to talk to him about his brother...

"What about Gabriel?" he sighed, pulling over the bowl of soup Marielle had brought in and handing it to Elina. She drank straight from the bowl with a serene, grateful expression, before growing serious once more.

"He hasn't gone missing. He ran off."

"...what?"

"I heard in the tavern," Elina continued. "The messenger who first came to tell you Gabriel was missing was talking to the town head. The war's been over for weeks, but he was keeping you in the dark to use the fighting on the border as a ruse to run off with a woman. Kilian, I'm so sorry - I should have believed you in the first place. He -"

"Gabriel really isn't coming back?"

Somehow the news stunned him, even though it was what Kilian had been thinking for weeks anyway. But it was one thing to believe something without any evidence. It was another thing entirely to find out that, all along, he'd been right to doubt his brother.

Gabriel had abandoned him, and it stung like nothing else ever had.

Elina clutched his hand. "Kilian, I'm so -"

"It's fine. I'm just glad you're okay. *I'm* the one who's sorry for telling you to leave."

She said nothing in response to Kilian's apology,

even though he never apologised to anyone. But she smiled, and that was all he had to see.

He ran a hand through his hair. "Guess I really am stuck here," he said, trying to keep his voice as even and casual as possible. "Guess I'm going to have to make peace with that fact before I freeze everyone to death."

Kilian wasn't expecting Elina's eyes to light up. She stared at him in earnest. "Kilian," she began, "do you think you could remember exactly what your father said and *how* he said it when he placed the curse on you?"

He frowned. "Yes...why?"

"Because I might have a magician that can help."

# Chapter Twenty-Three

***Elina***

It was an odd feeling, sitting in the strategy room of the Hale castle with Kilian, Scarlett Duke and Adrian Wolfe. Kilian was holding Elina's hand so tightly it almost hurt; he'd hardly let go of her since her brush with icy-cold death. It was reassuring, and gratifying, too, but it was also terrifying. It reminded Elina of just how close she'd stupidly come to killing herself...and what that would have meant. She'd have left her mother all alone. She'd have left *Kilian* alone, and he'd have never known what his brother had done.

Elina resolved to never act so rashly and stupidly ever again.

"So how did the two of you end up in such a miserable place like Alder in the middle of winter?" Kilian asked Scarlett and Adrian.

Scarlett smiled. "We've been travelling around for the past couple of years following rumours of magic. Most of the leads we followed turned out to be false.

Imagine our surprise when we met Elina and realised we had finally come across true magic!"

Kilian raised an eyebrow. "True magic from Elina?" He looked at her suspiciously. "I thought you didn't know any magic."

"Oh, she definitely doesn't," Adrian said, "but this castle is crawling with it. Her working here brought her in contact with it, so when we met her I could sense it."

"I find that hard to believe."

"And why is that?"

"I can't *feel* magic in here and I'm the one who's cursed."

Adrian laughed, his amber eyes bright with amusement. "That's because you don't know what it feels like. In time you would."

"I've been cursed for months, magician, is that not time enough?"

"Try years."

Kilian's eyes narrowed; even Elina looked at Adrian in surprise.

"You've been cursed for years?" she asked, curious.

"Yes," Adrian replied smoothly, as if the issue of being cursed didn't bother him whatsoever.

"What kind of –"

"A story for another time," Scarlett interjected. "I feel like the subject of your *own* curse, Your Royal Highness –"

"Call me Kilian."

"The subject of your own curse, Kilian, is far more

pressing," Scarlett finished. "Was your father definitely not touching anything when he cursed you?"

Kilian shook his head. "I wasn't facing him, and I was blind drunk, so I don't know. But I don't think so. The words were identical to the ones Elina's father spoke the first time, and *he* wasn't holding anything."

Adrian nodded. "Do you have anything of your father's?"

"Like a ring or a jacket?"

"No. Hair or bone or skin. Something *from* him."

Kilian thought carefully for a few moments, eyes staring sightlessly at the ceiling as he pondered the question. Then he nodded. "I'll be right back."

They waited for Kilian's return, Elina feeling curiously impatient. She wanted badly to know about Adrian's curse, and why he needed something of Kilian's father, and what their next move was going to be, and –

Kilian returned holding a familiar silver locket. He was staring at it with an odd expression on his face. "This was my mother's," he said. "She kept a lock of my father's hair in it. Stupidly sentimental. I suppose I'm glad of it now."

Then it seemed like a switch flicked on. He looked at Elina, then back at the locket. "The buttons on the overcoat you made me – the pattern on them matches this."

Elina's face reddened. "I may have found it when I was sneaking about the castle," she admitted sheepishly. "The pattern was so beautiful I couldn't help but replicate it. And it's not like I went rummaging through any drawers...it was just lying there on a table."

"I was looking at it myself earlier that day," Kilian mused, sitting down and handing the locket over to Adrian. "I don't know why."

"Maybe you're not so bad at sensing magic as you think," Adrian quipped, clicking open the locket and grasping the lock of hair between his fingers, a frown creasing his brow. It only deepened as time wore on.

"What is it?" Scarlett asked.

Adrian glanced at Kilian. "Give me some of your own hair."

Somewhat dubious, Kilian brought out a pocket knife and cut off a small quantity of hair from the bottom of his braid and handed it over to the other man.

After a few long moments of silence Adrian sighed. "Your father didn't curse you."

"I – what?"

"There's no magical link between the two of you. Your father had the spell cast on him, yes, but he isn't the one who transferred it to *you.*"

"How do you know that?" Elina asked.

"It's...complicated," Adrian admitted. "It's not easy to explain. But there's a link missing. The identity of the curse placed on Kilian doesn't match his father." He stared at Kilian. "Did you ever talk to your father about the curse after it was put on you?"

He shook his head. "I didn't speak to him at all. But that wasn't anything new – I avoided being in the castle as much as possible. I only stayed after the curse was put on me because I knew my father was going to die soon, and if I was anywhere else in the world when that happened then the curse would kill me for leaving the castle."

Nobody spoke for a while. Kilian, Scarlett and Elina all watched Adrian as he mulled over the unexpected problem at hand.

Eventually he asked, "Do you have anything of your brother's?"

No one needed this explained to them; the insinuation was obvious. Wordlessly Kilian left the room and returned a few minutes later with a brush laden with pale blonde strands of hair, handing it over to Adrian before sitting down.

It didn't take long before Adrian nodded. "It was Gabriel, no doubt about it."

Kilian banged a fist upon the table. "I don't understand! How did that happen – I thought that –"

"The only way to know what happened is to speak to your brother yourself."

"But he's run off!"

To everyone's surprise, Adrian shook his head. "He's about five miles away, and heading this way. Seems he hasn't run off as far as you think."

Kilian's mouth was wide in disbelief. "How do you know that?"

He waved the hairbrush. "There are perks to being a magician."

Elina squeezed Kilian's hand. "I guess you'll get your answers one way or another sooner rather than later."

But Kilian's face was blank; Elina couldn't tell what he was thinking at all.

“What am I supposed to do when he shows up, if he doesn’t tell me anything or simply leaves again?” he asked quietly. “If he has no intention of taking over then how can I force him to?”

Nobody answered.

Nobody knew.

# Chapter Twenty-Four

***Kilian***

"Are you sure you don't want me here with you?"

"No; I need to talk with him by myself."

Elina fussed with the buttons of Kilian's overcoat before he sat down on the throne. He was wearing the splendidly embroidered one Elina had made him, having finally thrown his old one in the fire. Paired with dark trousers, supple, leather boots, a clean-shaven face and his hair elegantly tied back, Kilian for once looked every inch a king.

All for a meeting with his brother, in which he'd have to try his hardest to push said role onto him. Kilian had no idea what to do or say; the whole endeavour seemed impossible.

The weather had cleared up since Kilian had warmed Elina back to life. She'd spent every night in the castle since then with him, and most of the daytime, too. It kept him settled and in control, even though Kilian rather felt like he might explode at any given moment.

But he couldn't have Elina with him when he spoke to his brother. It was something he had to do on his own if he wanted to settle things once and for all. That didn't make it any easier to watch Elina squeeze his hand, smile reassuringly at him and turn to leave, though; Kilian grabbed her wrist and pulled her back to him, landing a kiss upon her forehead without really thinking of what he was doing.

Elina glanced up at him through her eyelashes, the blush that spread across her cheeks unbearably pretty. "What was that for?" she asked softly.

"For nothing at all. For everything. Thank you, Elina."

When she broke away from him she rolled her eyes. "You don't have to keep thanking me for every little thing, Kilian. It's not like I'm going to disappear if you act like your usual, ungrateful, cynical self."

Kilian laughed into his hand before regaining his composure. "I suppose there's no point in acting like someone else around you. I have to at least *try* and appear level-headed and diplomatic if I'm to talk to Gabriel properly, though."

"So you're trying it out on me first?"

"No," he said. "I simply wanted to thank you."

Elina looked torn between leaving the throne room and returning to Kilian's side once more. "I'll be in the parlour room with Scarlett and Adrian in case you need me."

Kilian nodded.

And then Elina was gone, leaving him alone on the throne, pretending to be king. Kilian felt like he was going to be violently sick; his stomach was churning and his heart palpitating so badly he wished for alcohol to calm his nerves. But he persisted, keeping his back straight and his face calm when, finally, a knock on the door signalled the arrival of his brother.

Gabriel Hale looked regal even in the simple travelling clothes he was wearing as he entered the throne room. It was something about the way he held himself and walked with a purpose; when the two of them had been out in public Gabriel had always been recognised for what he was, whereas Kilian could slink off to a whorehouse without being noticed at all.

The brothers shared the pale eyes and even paler hair of their father, but Gabriel's jaw was more squared-off that Kilian's, and his cheekbones wider. He had a handsome face that screamed trustworthy. And Gabriel was just as even-tempered as their father had been. He never had a cruel word to say about anyone, and he was diplomatic to a fault in arguments. Everything about him was perfectly suited for being king.

Except that he had run away.

"Gabriel," Kilian drawled. "You don't look all that missing to me."

His brother grinned. "Well aren't you a sight for sore eyes up there, Kilian. You actually got dressed properly to greet me!"

He rolled his eyes. "Hardly. Where have you been? I've heard...conflicting reports about what's been going on at the borders. Is it true the fighting is over?"

Gabriel nodded. "There were some skirmishes I had to deal with that delayed the whole process, but yes. Thank you for dealing with those diplomats a few weeks back."

Kilian kept his suspicions from showing on his face. If the conversation Elina overheard was to be believed, then the fighting had been over weeks ago, and Gabriel was lying.

"I was informed that you were missing," he said, choosing his words very carefully. "I was worried."

Gabriel burst out laughing; the sound irked Kilian. "You, worried about me? I don't think so Kilian. I thought you were a better liar than that. I know you were only concerned about me taking the throne off your hands."

"And is that not what you've returned to do? You *are* the king, after all. And god knows nobody wants me to do it – least of all me. You know how useless I am."

Something flashed across Gabriel's face that Kilian didn't like the look of at all. He stared at his brother sitting on the throne and shook his head. "Maybe you *are* useless, Kilian, but it's because you never try. Can't you put some effort into something for once?"

"Why should I? I'm merely prince regent. The throne is yours, and now you're back."

"No, Kilian. I'm not."

"...excuse me?"

Gabriel ran a hand through his glossy hair. "This is a courtesy visit, brother. I won't be back. I have no intention of taking the throne – of being tied to it. My heart belongs elsewhere."

Kilian stood up immediately, pounding down the steps from the throne to reach his brother. Gabriel was taller than him; Kilian hated that he was. "I was never meant to be king," he seethed. "I'm not the one who should be trapped here."

"And yet you are. Father must have seen something –"

"*I know it was you!*" Kilian screamed. "I know it was you who cursed me, Gabriel!"

Gabriel seemed taken aback by this for a few moments, but then he schooled his expression and an easy smile crossed his lips. "I guess there's no point in asking how you know that. Either way, *you're* the one stuck in the castle, little brother. Not me."

Kilian glared at him. "Why did you do this to me? *How* could you do this to me?"

"Because father wouldn't," Gabriel explained. "I begged him to do it. I didn't want to stay here, on the mountainside. I wasn't ready to be trapped in the castle; I still had so much I wanted to do."

"And you think I didn't?!"

Gabriel laughed incredulously. "Tell me, Kilian, what have you ever done with your life? Nothing. Some responsibility will do you good."

"I don't want this!"

"And neither do I." Gabriel rounded on him, eyes glittering dangerously. "When father passed the curse on to me I guess he expected me to return from the borders as soon as I was sent word he was on his deathbed. For all he knew I *had* to, otherwise the curse would kill me. Tell me, how did he react when I never returned? Did he realise what I'd done – that I'd passed his damned magic on to you?"

Kilian looked away. "I didn't speak to him. I wasn't even there when he died."

The laugh that was emitted from Gabriel's mouth

was warped and cruel. "But of course you didn't. Classic, responsibility-shirking, closed-off Kilian at his finest. I suppose you get points for consistency, though had you only talked to father you'd have realised he never wanted you tied to the throne in the first place."

"You're...unbelievable," Kilian muttered. His hands were shaking; he curled them into fists. "Do you really think I'll let you leave the castle knowing all this?"

Gabriel shrugged. "And what can you do to keep me here? Nothing."

Kilian punched him in the face, but what he wasn't expecting was a sharp pain in his stomach in return. He looked down.

Gabriel had stabbed him.

"You...son of a bitch..." Kilian breathed.

"You won't die from something so minor, little brother," Gabriel said as he removed the knife and let it clatter to the floor. "I just need you incapacitated long enough for me to get far from here. Goodbye, Kilian."

Kilian didn't stay conscious long enough to watch his brother leave.

# Chapter Twenty-Five

*Elina*

When Elina found Kilian passed out on the floor of the throne room in a pool of blood she screamed. She'd never been one for raising her voice before, but in the past few days she'd found herself being louder than she ever had been. Shouting at Kilian. Wailing at the weather because of Kilian. Crying out *for* Kilian.

"Somebody help me!" she exclaimed, holding her hand to the wound in Kilian's stomach and putting as much pressure on it as she dared. On the floor by his side lay an ornate dagger, its intricately carved blade stained crimson. "Why wasn't anyone around to stop this?" she demanded when a couple of servants rushed into the room, followed by Scarlett and Adrian. "Why did nobody stop Gabriel?! Where is he?"

One of the servants looked back towards the doors. "He - we didn't know to stop him! We received no orders to detain him, and it's not as if Prince Kilian kept any personal guards in the castle - he got rid them all!"

Elina was too panicked to even be angry with Kilian for such a stupid move. Her eyes darted from Kilian's ashen face to the servants and back again. "Call a doctor. There must be one in the - oh, no. Don't say it."

They shook their heads sadly. "His Royal Highness let him go, too."

She almost pounded her fists on Kilian's chest. "You're an *idiot*!" she cried, not caring who heard her talk about the prince in such a way. But then Scarlett and Adrian knelt down beside her, and Scarlett calmly undid the buttons of Kilian's overcoat and removed it. Elina could hardly look at the dark fabric stained even darker with his blood.

"Elina, we'll handle this," Scarlett said. "Go ahead to Kilian's room and wait for us there."

"But -"

"Just do it," she interrupted firmly. Elina had never heard Scarlett speak in such a commanding tone before, but she wasn't in a position to protest. With one final, agonised look at Kilian's deathly pale face Elina got to her feet and stumbled to his chambers, flinging herself onto his bed when she reached it.

She wished there was a storm outside to mask the sounds of her crying, but outside it was eerily calm. Elina hated the silence. She hated what it insinuated.

"Don't you dare die, you coward," she muttered into a pillow. "Don't you dare."

*

Two hours passed before Kilian slowly came to. Adrian had propped him up in bed against several pillows; as soon as he began groaning and muttering Elina immediately roused from where she had been dozing, curled up beside him. She poured a glass of water and brought it to Kilian's lips before he'd even opened his eyes.

"I - hold on," Kilian spluttered weakly. He waved the water away. "Give me a minute. Ah, that hurts..." He looked down at his now tightly-bandaged stomach, mildly impressed. "Who patched me up? There's no doctor nearby."

"Scarlett did," Adrian replied. The woman in question was asleep in front of the blazing fire; nobody made a move to wake her. "Care to tell us what exactly happened, Kilian? Though I imagine it's not too difficult to put the pieces together."

Kilian took the glass of water from Elina and drank the entire thing before answering. "What I wouldn't give for that to be vodka," he joked, though his voice was strained as if trying to be funny physically hurt him. He took hold of Elina's hand, which was shaking. "I'm okay, Elina. Even Gabriel said I wouldn't die from the wound. I do not think he intended to kill me - merely to prevent me from going after him."

"That's - that's just as bad!" Elina cried, winding her fingers through Kilian's in a desperate attempt to get closer to him. She wished Scarlett and Adrian weren't in the room, so she could hide under the covers with Kilian and pretend the rest of the world didn't exist.

But that would solve nothing, even though it was all she could do personally for Kilian. Elina had never felt so useless.

Kilian smiled humourlessly. "Probably. Either way, he admitted to being the one who cursed me. He never wanted the throne, it seems. Clearly I should have tried harder to get to know my brother when I had the chance, then I might have seen this coming early enough to do something about it."

"Did he – did Gabriel say *why* he didn't want the throne?" Elina asked uncertainly. "Did he mention the woman he's supposed to have fallen for?"

"I didn't even get to ask about her. All Gabriel said was that he didn't want to be trapped here when he still had so much he wanted to see and do. It's not exactly a sentiment I don't share."

"But being king was *his* responsibility, not yours!"

Kilian stayed silent.

After a few moments Adrian spoke up, though he sounded very much like he didn't want to. "You know what you have to do to get out of this, don't you?"

"Does it really have to be this way?"

"The only other way to remove the curse is for another blood relative to take it on. You have none, other than Gabriel, and he's made it clear that he has no intention of holding the throne."

Elina stared at Adrian, confused. She narrowed her eyes. "What do you mean, Adrian? Kilian, what is it you have to do?"

Kilian hesitated. "I have to kill him. I have to kill my brother."

"No!" she cried, horrified. "Why? Adrian, surely there's something you can *do*? There must be another spell, or a counter-curse, or –"

"Elina, the magic your father performed was very, very complicated. I'm still struggling to work out exactly what he did, and how he did it. The surest way to remove a curse once and for all is to destroy the one who cast it...trust me, I know this all too well."

Adrian's eyes darted to Scarlett's sleeping figure as he spoke, and he was relieved to see she hadn't woken up. He smiled gently for Elina. "There is nothing else to be done about it. Kilian has to kill his brother."

"But, then..." Elina stared at her fingers entwined with Kilian's. "If you kill your brother to free you of the curse, who will then be king?"

Kilian laughed bitterly. "A problem for another day. I have to force Gabriel back to the castle first before we think about that." He stared out of the window, a frown shadowing his brow. "How long was I unconscious?"

"About two hours," Elina said. "Why?"

"Gabriel couldn't have gotten far in two hours with all the snow on the ground, even with the fair weather this afternoon. He should still be in range to feel the full brunt of a tempestuous little brother."

"Kilian?"

He grinned, eyes gleaming like the drunk madman Elina had first met. "Time to whip up one hell of a storm."

# Chapter Twenty-Six

***Kilian***

Kilian had never so viciously enjoyed being in control of the weather. Though Elina wouldn't let him leave his bed to sit by the window, he could still hear the horrendous noise of the storm and imagine the carnage it was causing just fine.

It hadn't been difficult for him to produce the storm. Kilian was in pain, and he was furious with his brother, as well as feeling betrayed. Part of him still couldn't quite believe Gabriel had stabbed him, even if it wasn't meant to be lethal.

*He came into the throne room knowing he'd have to do something like that to keep me from stopping him,* Kilian thought, barely keeping his temper in check at the memory of the cold, icy blade sliding into his stomach. *If I ever had any qualms about killing Gabriel before, I don't now.*

The plan was simple enough; if Gabriel was to have a hope of leaving the mountainside then he'd have to come and make his peace with Kilian. When he showed up, he'd be taken to Kilian's rooms to talk to him. Then, when he got close enough, Kilian would cut him with a knife coated in an evil-looking poison Adrian had given him. The blade would barely have to scratch the surface of Gabriel's skin; all the poison needed was one, tiny entryway to his bloodstream.

"Easy enough," Kilian muttered, stomach smarting when he tried to reposition himself in bed. Scarlett had done a superb job of tending to the stab wound – it wasn't even bleeding any more. But internally he was still suffering, and the plant extracts Kilian had been given to help with the pain were beginning to wear off.

*Good,* he thought. *Let the pain make the blizzard even worse.*

Four hours had passed since Kilian woke up. It was dark outside, and almost time for most people to retire to bed. Dully he thought that he'd rather like to join them in that regard; to fall back against the pillows with Elina in his arms, warm and safe and thinking of nothing but each other. But that was something to look forward to *after* the not-so-simple task of murdering his brother. Kilian grimaced at the thought.

*And then...*

He couldn't shake what Elina had asked upon finding out that Kilian would have to kill Gabriel. Who *would* be king once Kilian was free of the throne? Although he wanted nothing more than to run away and never think about it ever again, Kilian knew that he couldn't. Not if he wanted Elina to stay by his side and respect him as a human being. He couldn't leave the country in upheaval. He couldn't allow Alder to struggle through the next winter with no provisions put in place to help against awful mountainside weather.

When he heard a knock on the door Kilian flinched. “Who is it?”

A pause. “You know who it is, brother.”

Gritting his teeth against what was to come next, Kilian called out, “Come in, then.”

Gabriel was completely soaked through and half-covered in ice. When Kilian indicated towards a chair deliberately placed by his bedside, Gabriel instead headed straight for the fire to warm up his hands.

“I won’t apologise for what I did,” he said, back turned to Kilian as he basked in the heat from the flames.

“I wouldn’t expect you to. And yet you’re here because you have to ask me to let you leave, which stabbing me was supposed to prevent. Clearly you’re not as smart as you think you are.”

Gabriel chuckled. “Or perhaps I underestimated how petty you are, Kilian.”

“I wouldn’t call my reaction to being *stabbed* petty.”

“...I guess not. Let me leave, little brother.”

“And why should I?”

Gabriel left the heat of the fireplace to sit down in the chair by Kilian’s bed. He locked his eyes on his brother, running a hand through his sodden, frozen hair to push it away from his face.

“There’s a woman, Kilian,” he said very quietly. “I met her last year, at a ball. I never thought I’d see her again, but in summer she was travelling through our country. I spent some time with her, and fell completely in love with her. When the fighting broke out at the border I begged for her to go back to her home country, but she would not go. I wrote her so many letters before I was forced to travel down there myself."

Gabriel chuckled. "She's so stubborn. I knew I couldn't face never seeing her again, but I couldn't ask her to give up her freedom and live in this forsaken castle just for me, either. That's the main reason I passed the curse onto you, Kilian. If I hadn't I wouldn't have been able to be with the woman I love."

Kilian said nothing. His hand was wrapped around the handle of the poison-soaked knife. All he had to do was reach out and nick Gabriel's hand. But his brother's words were keeping him from moving, for of course he understood exactly how Gabriel was feeling.

"...did you not think I felt the same way, Gabriel?" Kilian asked, so softly his words were almost lost to the wind and the roar of the fire. "That I didn't want to be stuck here all alone?"

Gabriel eyed him awkwardly. "You – you've always been alone, Kilian. You never wanted to be with anyone, and that certainly didn't seem to change when you reached adulthood. You never loved anybody."

"That's not true, and you know it. Don't try to deflect responsibility by believing me incapable of love."

"Our parents are dead, Kilian. Who is there left for you?"

Kilian was overwhelmed by a wave of anger at such a remark. "You truly think I couldn't meet somebody new to care for?" he accused, eyes blazing. "Do you believe nobody would be able to put up with me long enough to care about me back? Is that it?"

"I..." Gabriel stared at his hands, then back at Kilian.

"Truthfully, yes. You're my brother, and I love you as best as I can, but you and I both know that you're not a good person."

"Then why would you have me be king?!"

"Because my love for Selene is greater than my love for my country."

Kilian frowned. "Is that her name? Selene? The woman you love?"

His brother nodded.

"It sounds Greek."

"That's because she *is* Greek."

And then, to Gabriel's surprise, Kilian burst out laughing. "How did we end up so similar when we're so different?"

Gabriel stared at him, expression dubious. "What on earth do you mean?"

"I'm in love with the magician's girl," Kilian said, closing his eyes and reclining his head against the pillow in stupid, nonsensical mirth. "I'm completely, shamelessly in love with her, and she's desperate to leave Alder, and I cannot go with her."

"You aren't...you're serious, aren't you?"

He nodded. "Of course I am. She's been by my side throughout the entire winter. I started acting more like a king for her. I stopped *drinking* for her. I fixed the weather for her. Not that any of that matters, ultimately."

"Kilian –"

"Just go, brother. Go back to your Selene and live the life you always wanted to have."

Even as Kilian spoke the words he hated himself.

He didn't want to be stuck in the castle forever. He wanted to kill his brother and be free of it all. He wanted to run away.

He simply couldn't do it.

For the first time in what felt like years, genuine affection spread across Gabriel's face. "Do you mean that?"

"No. Yes. Of course I do. I hate you, but I still can't force life imprisonment on you...even if you *did* stab me. So go. Don't let me see you again."

Gabriel smiled slightly. "I hope that last part isn't true. I would love for you to meet Selene one day. And I'd like to meet the magician's girl –"

"Don't push your luck," Kilian interrupted, waving his hand toward the door. "Just...go, Gabriel, before I change my mind and make it so cold outside you freeze to death where you stand."

When Gabriel ruffled his hair Kilian raised an arm to stop him. The knife was still in his hand; his brother stared at it sadly.

"You really did mean to kill me."

"I did before. You cannot blame me for it."

"...I guess I can't. I'll come back to see you in summer, Kilian. Try not to destroy the country before then."

"You don't get a say in the matter!" Kilian called out as his brother left the room. He sagged against the pillows, dropping the deadly knife to the floor. He'd lost all will to do anything.

*I guess this is my life now,* he thought, staring sightlessly at the window as the wind and snow and hail finally began to let up. *Maintaining my temper and being diplomatic for the sake of other people. Great.*

As Kilian drifted off to sleep he almost hoped that, come morning, he wouldn't wake up.

# Chapter Twenty-Seven

*Elina*

"You've done such an excellent job of fixing his overcoat, Elina."

"You'd never have known Kilian bled half to death wearing it."

"Adrian!"

Elina laughed softly. The three of them were sitting by the fire in her mother's house, drinking wine whilst Elina finished up the repairs to Kilian's overcoat. When her mother came in with a tray of food both Adrian and Scarlett's eyes lit up.

"Thank you, Lily!" Scarlett exclaimed, which was echoed by Adrian. The two of them had grown close to Lily during their stay in Alder; Elina suspected they talked about her mother's affair with the magician as well as digging up old and embarrassing stories about Elina herself. She was glad for it; her mother relished the company.

"Don't mention it," Lily said, sitting down in her favourite chair by the fire before being handed a goblet of wine from Adrian. "You really have done a wonderful job repairing the coat, Elina," she remarked as she observed the fabric. "When you brought it back to the shop my heart almost broke in two. You worked so hard on it."

"Yes, well, it was just about the only thing I managed to do of use for Kilian," she muttered.

Elina hadn't wanted Kilian to kill his older brother. That didn't change how distraught she was that Kilian was now stuck forever in a castle he hated, doing a job he'd never wanted in a country he was desperate to escape from. He'd given up everything for his brother's happiness, even after what Gabriel had done to him. It wasn't something Elina could understand, since she had no siblings herself, so all she could do was respect Kilian's decision and support him.

He hadn't unceremoniously kicked Elina, nor Scarlett and Adrian, from his castle after Gabriel left. But Kilian also hadn't spoken much, choosing instead to sleep and keep to himself, so the three of them had returned to Alder three days after he'd let his brother go. Elina wanted nothing more than to stay by Kilian's side and tell him everything would be fine, but she knew it was a lie.

Nothing was fine. And, if Elina was being honest, she wasn't sure if she had it in her to stay in Alder the rest of her life for Kilian's sake. He certainly wouldn't allow her to in the first place – Kilian had made that much very clear from the moment he'd first heard Gabriel was missing. It demonstrated just how much he'd grown as a person, even if Kilian would deny such growth.

It only made Elina feel worse.

Adrian gently kicked her ankle, knocking her out of her reverie. "There's nothing you can do, Elina, short of chasing after Gabriel and killing him on Kilian's behalf."

Elina made a face. "Don't tempt me."

Scarlett sighed into her wine. "It's not fair. On anyone. Your country will suffer from having a king who does not wish to lead, and their dissent will in turn negatively affect Kilian. And that's not even touching upon the personal issues the curse brings up. I don't think Kilian will last all that long locked up."

"The only reason he's still alive is that he's been too much of a coward to kill himself," Elina admitted, a cold shiver crawling up her spine despite the heat from the fire. "Something tells me he's becoming less of a coward with every passing day...and that's not a good thing."

From her chair in the corner Lily watched her daughter with an expression full of sympathy. "Elina, he might yet prove to be stronger than you all think he is. Didn't he properly work with those diplomats before? The ones that *actually* ended the fighting?"

Elina nodded. "But I had to *force* him to speak to them."

Her mother smiled. "But even so, Kilian did do his job. And he chose not to kill his brother, even though that meant tying himself to the position of king. I think he's far more magnanimous than any of us have given him credit for."

"Mama, that's not the problem," Elina said, head drooping sadly. "Kilian could pour his heart and soul into being a good king – and actually manage it – but that doesn't change the fact that he's trapped in the castle.

He can't even go out into the castle grounds! And the weather entirely depends on him keeping level-headed. Kilian...he was already halfway to madness when I met him. Being cooped up for the rest of his life will only make things worse."

There was silence in the room for a long time after that, for Elina spoke the truth. They could all try their best to help with improving Kilian's circumstances within the boundaries that had been set, but that didn't change how restrictive those boundaries were in the first place.

Eventually Lily downed her wine and allowed Adrian to pour her another glass. "If only Alesandro were here."

Elina stared at her. "Who's Alesandro?"

"Why, your father, of course. Have I – have I never told you his name before?"

"No," Elina said, shaking her head. "And everyone in town called him 'the magician'. I had no idea."

"That's...I'm sorry I never told you, Elina."

Elina waved a dismissive hand. "It doesn't matter. He's not my *father* anyway."

"And yet his blood runs through you nonetheless."

A smash by the fireplace caught them both by surprise; Scarlett had dropped her goblet on the hearth, spilling burgundy wine and glass all over the floor. She was staring at Adrian with wide eyes, which he returned with a look of baffled understanding.

"Of course," he murmured, scratching his chin before beginning to pick up the shards of glass from the floor as if in a trance. "Scarlett, why didn't we think of that before?"

"We were too set on the curse itself. And this wouldn't even be a counter-spell. It's just a...coincidental curse."

Lily and Elina glanced at each other in confusion before setting their eyes on Adrian. "What are you two talking about? What would be a coincidental curse?"

Adrian grinned wolfishly. "Elina, do you think you could cope staying by the king's side for the rest of his life?"

# Chapter Twenty-Eight

***Kilian***

Kilian was staring out the window again. This time, however, he wasn't in his own chambers but in the ballroom. The large, expansive windows along the southern wall faced the back gardens of the castle, much like the dining room windows did. He watched sightlessly as the water in the hot springs bubbled and rose as steam, a keening sense of longing filling the pit of his stomach.

He'd largely recovered from the physical trauma of being stabbed, though the mental trauma of the act was something Kilian doubted he'd ever fully get over. He had been the *better person.* He had been the bigger man to his brother, who had always been the golden son.

And he'd been punished for it.

With a sigh he rolled off the windowsill, stalking across the ballroom floor towards the exit. He thought of his and Elina's midnight dance as his footsteps echoed off the walls. It felt like it had happened a thousand years ago when, in truth, it was barely three weeks ago.

*So much can happen in so short a space of time,* he thought, sighing once more as he made his way up the grand staircase. Kilian didn't really know where he was going - he didn't want to return to his chambers, which were beginning to feel suffocating. He wasn't hungry. He didn't feel like striking up a conversation with any of the servants, nor reading a book in the parlour room. In frustration he collapsed onto the second-from-bottom stair, leaning against the railing as he stared dispassionately at the main doors into, and out of, the castle.

Kilian thought of finding Elina by them, half-frozen to death. If she hadn't literally fallen through the gap in the open door onto the castle floor then Kilian would not have been able to drag her inside.

"How stupid," he muttered, a horrible shudder wracking his body at the thought of having not been able to save Elina because of her father's curse. His stomach twinged in pain; Kilian bent over double until it subsided.

He had no idea how long he sat on the stairs, silent and alone. There was no wind nor snow nor rain to interfere with the quiet, though the sky remained permanently overcast with thick, grey cloud. Kilian could just about control his temper enough to keep the storms at bay, but he was too miserable to let the sun through. He wondered if he'd ever see it again.

When a loud knock on the front door reverberated around the hall, it took Kilian a moment to respond.

"Who is it?" he called out, leaving the staircase to stand by the heavy wood-and-iron door.

"Kilian?" a familiar but muffled voice exclaimed back. Elina. "What are you doing standing by the door?"

"I don't know."

"Are you going to let me in?"

Kilian considered this for a moment. He knew he had to end things with Elina before it became impossible for him to do so. She needed to be free of any and all lingering responsibility towards him in order to leave Alder and finally live her life. But if he never saw her then he never had to end things, so Kilian seriously considered telling her to leave.

"I can practically hear what you're thinking, *Your Royal Highness,*" Elina said sarcastically.

"Technically it's Your Majesty, now," he quipped back. He drooped his head in resignation as he struggled to open the heavy door. "Fine; you can come in."

Elina was stark and beautiful against the snow, in a green dress the colour of pine needles that was astounding layered over the golden tones of her skin. In her arms was a familiar box.

"I come bearing gifts," she announced. "Well, the same gift as before. I repaired your coat."

"I thought you didn't have a green dress," Kilian said, frowning when Elina made no move to enter the castle. "Aren't you going to come in? It's cold by the door."

"I never said I didn't have a green dress – only that I didn't want to wear green," she replied, decidedly avoiding Kilian's question. She twirled on the spot, allowing the skirt of her dress to spin around her. "Do you like it? My mother made it for my eighteenth birthday. I can't believe I was too self-conscious about the way I looked to wear it. Seems pointless now."

Kilian crossed his arms. "It's lovely. Now come in. I can't feel my fingers."

She flashed a mischievous smile. "Why don't you come out here and let me warm them up?"

"Are you drunk, Elina? How could I leave the castle?"

"Just try it."

"No."

"Do it for me."

"Elina," Kilian complained, running a hand over his face in exasperation. "I'm not in the mood for whatever game it is you're playing."

But Elina's face had turned serious. "I'm not playing a game. Try and take a step outside, Kilian."

"Elina –"

"Please."

Kilian felt wretched. Whatever it was Elina was hoping for wasn't going to work. After all, what had changed? Absolutely nothing. But clearly it was important to her, so reluctantly he edged his feet to the door's threshold. He looked at Elina. "I'm not wearing shoes."

She shrugged. "Doesn't matter. Just try it."

Kilian's heart sped up despite himself, thinking that what he was about to do was incredibly stupid. As soon as he reached out to take a step some invisible force would prevent him from doing so, and that would be the end of it. He inched a foot forward.

Nothing happened.

Frowning, Kilian tentatively took a step out onto the snow, and then another. There was no hook pulling him back inside, nor a wall stopping him moving forward. No, there was only freezing, biting snow beneath his feet, urging him to walk faster and faster until he reached Elina's side.

He stared at her in wonder. "What happened? What did you – what did you do, Elina?"

She beamed. "Adrian and Scarlett have cursed me."

"They've – what?!" Kilian sputtered. "Have you lost your mind?"

Elina merely laughed. "It's nothing bad. In fact, I'd say it's fairly wonderful."

"...what did they do to you?"

"It was my mother's idea, technically," Elina explained, opening the box in her arms and taking out the beautiful overcoat she'd made for Kilian before passing it over to him. He dutifully shrugged it on. "She said something about me having my father's blood. Magician's blood."

"I don't understand," Kilian complained. "I thought we already established you don't possess any magical ability?"

"No, but I still contain the blood of the one who created the spell cast upon the Hale family," she said. "So Adrian managed to weave some...balancing magic, if you will, against your curse. Or maybe 'neutralising' is a better word for it." Elina seemed to ponder this for a moment before shaking her head. "Either way, it negates your own curse. There's only one condition."

"I don't like the sound of that. Elina, I don't want you to have to give up anything for my –"

"Let me finish, Kilian," she laughed. "The condition is that I have to stay by your side. The spell is distance-sensitive, so I can't be further than a few metres away from you in order to keep your curse at bay. Adrian thinks up to ten, maybe, but told me not to push it –"

Kilian cut her off with his mouth upon hers. He couldn't believe what he was hearing. The curse put on him would be lifted *and* Elina would stay with him? Moreover, Elina was the literal reason he could be free of everything in the first place?

"You'd really stay with me for me to be free?" he asked, voice trembling as tears filled his eyes. Kilian didn't care if he looked weak. Not in front of Elina.

She brought a hand up to cup his cheek; above them the sun just barely managed to break through the clouds, lighting the very edges of her hair on fire and adding gold to the green of her eyes. "Of course I'll stay by your side, Kilian. You love me, don't you?"

He choked on a laugh. "*I* love *you?* And what about the other way around?"

Elina wrinkled her nose. "That's up for debate. I guess you'll have to put up with me first and find out."

"This really isn't all a dream? This is really happening?"

"Yes, you idiot."

"Then for the love of god can we get back inside? Otherwise I'll have no feet left with which to wander the world with you."

Elina's lips curled into a sly smile.

"Yes, Your Majesty."

# Epilogue

***Elina***

"That's – Your Majesty! Oh my – Gill, get the good wine out! Your Majesty, I –"

"I'd prefer vodka, if you have it," Kilian said mildly, his expression blatantly amused at the looks of shock on the faces of everyone in the tavern. When Elina spied her mother, Scarlett and Adrian sitting at the back of the tavern she linked an arm through Kilian's and wound him through the throng of stunned townspeople.

To her right she spied Daven, staring at her in amazement. She felt just a tinge of guilt that she had not yet properly rejected him. Hopefully walking into the tavern in arm with the literal king would let him down better than Elina ever could with words.

"So you have deigned to drink with the commoners, Your Majesty?" Adrian drawled, face flushed from alcohol. He was clearly rather drunk; Scarlett swatted his arm good-naturedly.

"Careful about what you say when you're drunk.

You don't want a repeat of last time when that witchdoctor turned you back into a –"

Adrian laughed the rest of Scarlett's sentence away, just a tinge of embarrassment colouring the red of his cheeks. Elina was deathly curious.

"What were you turned into?" she asked, just as Gill herself brought over an ice-cold bottle of vodka to their table, along with a very good bottle of red wine.

"On the house, of course," she said, her face growing redder than Adrian's when Kilian beamed at her. With his perfect cheekbones, crystal-blue eyes, immaculately-braided hair and expensive clothes it was no wonder Gill was besotted with the sight of him. Out of the corner of her eye Elina spied most of the women of Alder looking at him longingly.

"I preferred you when you were scruffy," she muttered, so quietly only Kilian could hear.

He grinned. "Are you jealous, Elina? Because I'd rather say *I'm* jealous of the way all the men were looking at you when we entered here."

Elina rolled her eyes. "They were not."

She cried out in surprise when Kilian snaked a hand through her hair and pulled her in for a long, lingering kiss. When he let go his eyes were glittering in amusement. "Well, just in case, now they all know both of us are unavailable."

"You...behave yourself!" Elina pushed him away and grabbed a goblet of wine, face unbearably hot with the knowledge that most everyone was looking at her. But it was a good kind of embarrassment. She was pleased that Kilian had absolutely no qualms in demonstrating his affection for her in front of everyone.

"And for the record, magician," Kilian said as he settled down onto a chair, throwing a shot of vodka down his throat before continuing, "I very rarely drank with people of the same station as me. I was far more likely found passed out in whorehouses or seedy taverns hidden down back alleys or –"

"Kilian, everyone is listening to you!"

He glanced around the tavern and, sure enough, each and every person in the building was attentively listening to his every word. Kilian shrugged. "It's hardly as if my social proclivities were unknown. And besides, I won't be king for much longer anyway."

"Oh?"

It was Lily who had spoken, who until now hadn't met a grown-up Kilian. He smiled, standing up only to kneel in front of her and kiss her hand. Her eyes widened in shock.

"Miss Brodeur, I have a great deal to thank you for. For bringing Elina into the world when everyone else would have suggested otherwise. For raising her to be the kind of woman who wouldn't let me get away with throwing my life away. For instilling in her the desire to do more than simply live in Alder. But, most of all...I wish to apologise."

Lily looked down at him uncertainly, the blush that spread across her cheeks making her look far younger than she was. In that moment Elina saw the beautiful woman who had raised her – the one who had seduced, and been seduced by, a mysterious magician.

"What could you possibly have to apologise to me for, Your Majesty?" she asked politely.

Kilian's gaze was steady as he said, "Once upon a

time a wonderful woman spun a spoiled, angry little boy a set of clothes that were far too good for him. The boy set them ablaze, for no reason other than the fact that he could. It was certainly not one of his finer moments."

Lily laughed. "Please get up, Your Majesty. All is forgiven. I'm happy enough to see you wearing clothes from my family at all, even if it took you twenty-one years to accept them."

He glanced down at his blue-and-gold overcoat before looking at Elina. "Your entire family are certainly very talented. So, tell me, Miss Brodeur, I heard that you're looking to travel with your daughter come spring. Would you be entirely averse to a third person joining the party? I've always wanted to visit Greece."

Lily frowned, as did several people in the tavern. "Your Majesty, I don't understand. How can you come travelling when you have a country to run?"

When Kilian caught Frederick's eye, the man stood up. Elina struggled to hold back a smile; Kilian had thought long and hard about what to do with regards to the crown.

"Over the coming months I'll be working with representatives from each of the major towns to form a democratic government," he announced, for the whole tavern to hear. "I think it's about time our country moves away from a monarchy; it's outdated and... problematic." He shared a glance with Elina, who laughed into her hand at the understatement.

"I think most everyone - particularly in Alder - can agree that I'm not fit to sit on the throne," Kilian continued. "I would be far more comfortable knowing that I have absolutely nothing to do with the maintenance of an entire country. This does mean, however...”

There was a general air of uncertainty at this final sentence. Elina almost hit Kilian for pausing for dramatic effect, especially when he knocked back another shot of vodka.

“This does mean that there’s nothing protecting the country from a harsh winter. We’ll have to work collectively to ensure that what happened twenty years ago does not repeat itself. We cannot be unprepared for such horrific weather again. There will be no magician protecting the land. No mild-mannered king controlling the skies for your benefit. No curses or spells or enchantments making us special.”

The room was silent for a few moments, and then it erupted in an overwhelming wave of noise.

“I *knew* the curse was real!”

“The king really was controlling the weather? That’s insane!”

“Does that mean Prince Kilian - King Kilian - was responsible for the awful weather over the past few months?”

“Hey, keep your mouth shut. He’s right there...”

Kilian merely laughed at the comment before turning his attention back to Elina and the rest of the table. She stopped him from picking up another glass of vodka.

“Pace yourself, Mister Alcoholic.”

“I can handle *three* measures of vodka, Elina.”

She quirked an eyebrow. “On your own head be it. But if you pass out in the forest on the way back through to the castle it won’t be my fault.”

"At least the two of you might actually make it that far," Scarlett complained, struggling beneath a now unconscious Adrian happily dozing on her shoulder. "We're supposed to be leaving in the morning! There's no way Adrian will be willing to go anywhere with the hangover he'll doubtlessly have come sunrise. If only he could still turn into a wolf, we could have left tonight."

Kilian and Elina stared at her in shock. Lily, however, looked unperturbed; clearly she was privy to Scarlett and Adrian's full history.

"Did you say *wolf*?" Elina exclaimed.

Scarlett nodded.

"As in...an actual wolf," Kilian added, "not some metaphorical wolf?"

She nodded again. "It's a very, very long story. Perhaps one for the next time we cross paths."

"And when would that be? How are we supposed to find you?"

"Oh, I have no doubt we'll find *you,*" Scarlett said, smiling mysteriously. "We have your hair after all, Kilian."

He scratched his head. "You can curse me using that, can't you?"

"Do you really want the truth?"

"...no."

"Then we can't curse you using it," she laughed.

Elina and Kilian glanced at each other, slow, sheepish smiles spreading across their faces. Even though they had managed to free Kilian from the throne, and negated his curse, and Elina had finally made peace with her father being the magician who set everything off in the first place, that didn't mean they were free from the touch of magic. It would likely follow them wherever they went.

But, for the first time in their lives, they could finally accept that.

# Extra Chapter

***Kilian***

"Kilian, it's still too cold to use the hot springs and you know it."

"Hence why we need to get into the water as soon as possible."

Kilian didn't wait for Elina's retort; he threw her unceremoniously into the water, clothes and all. When she broke the surface, spluttering and gasping for air, she glared at him.

"I didn't bring a spare set of clothes. I'll freeze on my way back to the castle."

"You can wear my coat," Kilian replied simply, sliding out of his clothes quickly before stepping into the bubbling water himself. His mouth slid into a grin. "Or you could return naked. I'd rather like to see that."

Elina made a wave of water with her hand and sent it crashing towards him. "As if I'd do that. I'm worried that if the weather stays like this our journey down to Greece will be delayed."

Kilian shrugged. "That's what happens when one can no longer control the weather. Blizzards in March. Sleet for rain. Beautiful."

"Maybe I should keep my distance from you just to give the roads a chance to clear..." Elina muttered, turning away from Kilian as she spoke. He pulled her back to him, sitting her on his lap and biting her lip when Elina cried out in surprise.

"If you stayed far enough away to keep me trapped in the castle then the weather would get *worse,* I'd wager," Kilian said. He kissed her softly. "Are you so sick of me already, Elina?"

She rolled her eyes, then pushed away from Kilian in order to swim a few curious strokes across the pool. "You'd know it if I was, Your Majesty."

"I'm not –"

"You *are,* at least until those documents up in your office are completed and signed," Elina countered, causing Kilian to sigh.

He knew he had to finish looking them over. He knew he had to sign them. Kilian simply...couldn't be bothered. *This is precisely why I'm demolishing the throne, of course,* he thought as he relaxed against the side of the hot springs. For how could he face sitting in an office, worrying over paperwork, when instead he could content himself with watching Elina swim through clouds of steam and swirling snow?

*She still has her clothes on. That needs to change.*

"Take off your dress," Kilian complained, waving a hand in Elina's general direction as he did so. "The water feels much better against naked skin, you know."

"Oh, so it's not simply because you want me to undress for your own benefit?"

"I never suggested I didn't think that, too."

Elina paused in the middle of the pool, reaching her toes down to touch the smooth stone surface beneath her before unlacing the front of her dress. Her eyes never left Kilian's as she did so, her expression torn between amusement and exasperation.

"Let down your hair," Kilian insisted, after Elina was blessedly freed from her clothing.

She shook her head. "Absolutely not. That will definitely cause me to freeze on the way back to - *Kilian*!"

Kilian lunged for her, sliding an arm around Elina's neck to drag her below the surface of the water. He wrapped his legs around her waist, keeping her firmly in place as he unfurled the braid she had pinned around her head with deft fingers. When he finally let Elina go she kicked him away, outraged.

"You can't just - what sort of manners do you have to push a woman down into a body of water, Kilian?" she demanded, the moment she broke through the water once more.

He didn't answer; he didn't have to. They both knew he had less than no manners until it benefited him to pretend he had some. Instead, Kilian watched with growing hunger as Elina's wavy, tawny hair spread out around her golden shoulders in the water, rippling and undulating like it was made of magic.

"You look like a mermaid," he said, taking another few paces back in order to truly appreciate the sight of Elina in all her naked, ethereal splendour. Kilian didn't think he'd ever grow tired of the sight of her, especially against a backdrop of snow and steam and hot, bubbling water. They were the very foundation upon which he had gotten to know her. Upon which he'd fallen in love with her.

A small, pleased smile curled Elina's lips. She glanced downward at her hair winding its way all around her through the water. "Have you seen a mermaid before, to compare me to such a thing?"

"If I said I had, would you believe me?"

"No."

Kilian chuckled. He swam across to the other side of the pool, then back over to Elina's side. "You're right not to believe me. I don't even *know* if you look like a mermaid. They might be horrific, ugly creatures to look upon. They might be green. They might be –"

"I'm surprised, Kilian," Elina interrupted, raising an eyebrow. "It's unusual to hear you actually interested in something. To want to *know* something that serves you no benefit in knowing."

Kilian could only laugh. "I guess you're right. It would be unusual if I didn't become at least a little fascinated with all things strange and magical after everything I've been through, though. Don't you agree?"

"Are you honestly asking if 'the magician's girl' understands your interest in magic?"

"You never seemed that inclined to understand it."

"That was before," Elina muttered. She lowered her head into the water and exhaled a stream of bubbles. When she resurfaced she sighed. "I never wanted to be associated with my father, remember? But things are different now. And what with us leaving for Greece soon...”

Kilian placed a hand beneath Elina’s chin, turning her head to look at him. Her winter-forest eyes looked decidedly uncertain.

“We do not have to seek out your father if it scares you,” he said, not unkindly. “We can venture down with your mother and then head off on our own adventure once she’s safely in Greece. Nobody will force you to –”

“But that’s the thing,” Elina cut in. “I *do* want to meet him. I want to get to know him. I want to know... why he never came to see my mother again.”

Kilian frowned. “Did he know about her pregnancy?”

“Mama said she wasn’t sure,” she replied. “She never told him, but he was a magician. He had his ways, probably.”

“We should have asked Adrian if it were possible for him to work out such a thing, then we wouldn’t have to speculate.”

“Yes, well it’s not as if we thought to ask questions like that before he and Scarlett left,” Elina said. She removed Kilian’s hand from below her chin in order to arch her neck back to stare up at the wild, white, evening sky. “I wonder when we’ll see them again.”

Kilian joined her in looking upwards. “Scarlett certainly made it out like it wouldn’t be long. Though the woman is rather mysterious so who knows what she actually meant.”

“I guess we’ll just have to wait and find out.”

Elina smiled. “I guess we have to do a lot of that. Waiting and finding out, I mean. About Scarlett and

Adrian. About my father. About whether the country will be fine without a king."

"And whether I murder Gabriel next time I see him for being an arrogant, all-knowing piece of –"

Elina's mouth on Kilian's swallowed the rest of his sentence. "We both know you'd never do anything of the sort," she said, her words whisper-soft against Kilian's lips. "Just imagine him arriving to visit you in summer, instead, only to find you gone and the monarchy entirely erased."

The thought elicited a rough, throaty laugh from Kilian. How he would love to see the look on his brother's face upon discovering that Kilian was no longer tied to the throne. That Kilian – and people who *cared* for Kilian – had discovered a way to get around the Hale curse that Gabriel had not.

"I've been wondering for a while now about something," Elina murmured, after a few moments of her doing nothing but planting affectionate yet absent-minded kisses on Kilian.

"What is it you've been wondering about?" He pulled her closer against him, revelling in the feeling of every inch of Elina's wet, hot skin on his. He was very close to wishing to talk no longer in favour of something far more physical.

She kissed the end of his nose. "Once there's no longer a king, will your curse still stand? Or will it be negated entirely? It's hardly as if you father asked mine about the hypotheticals of the curse before having it placed."

Kilian paused to consider this for a moment. He grinned. "I guess we'll have to –"

"Wait and find out," Elina finished for him, giggling softly.

"Speaking of," he said, sliding a hand down to Elina's thigh to hitch her leg around his waist, "I've been very patient since we got into the hot springs, but I'm done with *waiting*."

Elina blushed and looked away, though she was smiling. "And what would that be for?"

"You."

***

Continue the Chronicles of Curses series with The Tower Without a Door.

# Chronicles of Curses Book Three - The Tower Without A Door

*Genevieve*

Today marked the end of Genevieve's twelfth solitary year, which coincided with her birthday. Twenty years since her birth, and more than half of those spent with nobody to touch or talk or listen to. She no longer wasted her time - though she had so much of it - wondering why she had been spirited away to the tower in which she now lived. For it was a pointless endeavour, as there were no answers to any of Genevieve's questions.

"What do you think we've been sent for breakfast today, Evie?" she asked aloud the moment she'd woken up and stretched her arms above her head. Genevieve was a troublesome mouthful of a name, especially if one was going to talk to herself. 'Evie' was much better.

Evie talked to herself a lot. What else was she supposed to do when there was nobody else to talk to? When she was first sent to the tower and discovered food and supplies magically appeared there twice a day Evie had hoped she'd eventually meet the person responsible for doing so.

Twelve years later and there was still no sign of the elusive person.

When she was a child, back in her father's palace, there had been a wizard. They'd gone to war together back before her father took the throne. The man was the most powerful wizard Evie knew...not that she knew any other wizards, of course, but if he worked side-by-side with the king then Evie could only assume he was the strongest. She had never known his name, for she hadn't been allowed to speak to the wizard nor ask after him. But she heard people call him The Thorn Wizard, so that's what she'd called him, too.

Evie had wondered for a while, back when she was eight and nine and even ten years old, if Thorn was the one sending her food. She was sure he was the one who'd sent her to the tower in the first place, so it made sense to her child's brain that he was making sure she didn't starve.

"None of it makes sense," Evie murmured as she rummaged through the basket that had appeared whilst she was sleeping. "Not a single thing."

The food inside was the usual - bread and cheese and apples and a few slices of cured meats. A pitcher of water. Nothing out of the ordinary. No cake or pastries or anything special to mark her birthday. Most of her meals consisted of similar fare, and it was never enough. Either the person sending Evie food still believed her to be eight years old or they were cruel. She was *twenty,* and needed an adult's portion of food.

Because of this Evie was on the skinny side, and was shorter than she remembered her mother being. But she hadn't seen the woman in twelve years; for all Evie knew she was actually of a height with her now.

It wasn't just food she was hungry for. No, what Evie craved was knowledge. Of what happened on the eve of her eighth birthday that resulted in her being sent to live in an enchanted tower with no door. Of how far she was from Willow, and the palace, and her family. Of whether any of her family were still alive at all. Of what lay outside the solitary window that was Evie's only proof that a world out with her tower in fact existed.

She padded over to the windowsill even now to look outside, bringing with her the basket of food to pick it apart with mindless, fidgeting fingers. Evie allowed her hair to hang out of the window, if only because it was the one part of her that could.

For Evie's hair was so long it now trailed on the floor behind her feet when she walked. She might have cut it, if there had been something sharp in the tower to cut it with. But all she had at her disposal was a bed, a bathroom, a table and tall, near-endless bookshelves. They didn't seem so endless now that Evie was twenty; she had read most every book on them, and some of the tomes more than once.

None of those things could be used to cut her hair. Evie had considered using a candle to burn it, once, but she scared herself out of doing it. One of her most treasured memories of her mother had been of her combing her golden hair, singing softly all the while, until Evie's locks were soft and shiny and lustrous.

*I looked after it as best I could, mama,* Evie thought, glancing down to where its ends hung several feet below the windowsill. Sometimes she would spend an hour or two braiding it into elaborate hairstyles that she found in books; usually Evie let it hang loose and free and bothersome.

She gnawed off a hunk of bread and slumped her shoulders as she chewed. It was a beautiful early summer's day. The sun shone brightly in the sky promising that, by midday, any sensible person would be seeking shade from its glaring rays. It lit up every strand of Evie's hair until it looked like it really *was* made of gold. It was one of her favourite things to see.

Below her - far, far below her - was a sloping, grassy meadow that met a forest on its right hand side. The trees along the closest edge were broad and low-boughed and lost their leaves in autumn. But she could see further into the forest from the height of her tower, where the trees were dark and evergreen. It looked dangerous and foreboding.

Evie longed to explore it.

Perhaps it was because this was her twentieth year. Perhaps it was because she wanted to get back to her family and find out why she'd been sent away. Perhaps it was because all of her clothes were too small and she was always hungry. Perhaps it was because she had run out of books to read.

Whatever the reason, today was the day Princess Genevieve was going to escape from the tower, or die trying.

She hoped she wouldn't die trying.

Evie had shredded any clothes she'd been sent over the past twelve years - save for one or two dresses to actually wear - in order to weave the fabric into ropes. She'd learned how to make them properly from one of the books in the tower. Individually they more than supported her weight.

But now they were all tied together in order to make a rope whose end dangled about five metres above the meadow, and she had to hope it would support her weight until she reached the final inches of it. Evie didn't relish the fact she'd have to brace for a fall to the grass. She'd probably break an arm or an ankle; she hoped she'd be able to use the rough stone surface of the tower to climb down the last few metres instead.

There was a lot of *hoping* going on in this plan.

But Evie was nothing if not an optimist, and if she stayed in the tower for much longer she'd likely die of boredom or loneliness, anyway.

"Or I might starve to death," she posed to the air, sighing dramatically as she finished her meagre breakfast. But Evie knew she was just as likely to slowly waste away until she was old, when time itself would finally - finally - give her an escape from her living hell.

An optimist, indeed.

With nothing left to lose, Evie tucked her hair behind her ears and grabbed her makeshift rope. A lurching in her stomach as she approached the window once more told her that she was definitely not as confident about her plan now that she actually had to follow it through.

"You have nothing to lose but yourself," Evie breathed, closing her eyes for a few moments whilst she tried in vain to settle the erratic beating of her heart. Then she tied the rope to one of her bedposts, checked its stability by tugging on it several times, dropped the rest of the rope through the window, and -

"Oh my oh my oh my, I can't do this," Evie cried, the moment she tried to position herself on the windowsill to abseil down the tower. She clung to the rope in terror, forcing her weight backwards until the only part of her body still in contact with the tower was her bare feet. She'd never been sent shoes once in twelve years. But, then again, who needed shoes when they were locked up inside a single room?

With all the strength of will she could muster, Evie dragged her feet downward an inch. Two. Three. Already her arms were protesting against supporting her weight on a rope that was beginning to chafe the skin of her hands.

And then she slipped. Evie fell two feet in absolute terror, screaming, before she managed to wrap her legs around the rope to hold herself in place. It felt like her muscles were made of water; any moment now they would give way and Evie would fall to the ground below and perish.

She sobbed, closing her eyes to the world as if that would somehow make everything go away. "I can't do it I can't do it I can't do it I'm going to die I'm going to – *ah*!"

For at the very moment that Evie felt her hands losing their grip once more, a much stronger pair of hands grabbed the rope from above her and yanked her back to the windowsill. She kept her eyes closed until the same pair of hands pulled her through the window and roughly threw her to the floor.

Evie's heart had been throbbing before; it was nothing compared to how painful it was now. She'd nearly died, and for what? Managing to climb down all of three feet from the tower window – two of which had only been achieved through falling?

It took Evie a few seconds before her brain finally kicked in and reminded her that someone had saved her life.

Someone. A person. A human being.

She flung her eyes open.

A man stood there, face covered in stubble with hair overgrown across his eyes. A ragged cloak hung from his shoulders, obscuring the rest of his tall frame. Though Evie couldn't see his face properly she had the overwhelming feeling that he was glaring at her.

She didn't speak. She didn't know what to say. All she could do was stare.

The man bent low to regard her. Evie, tangled in her hair and the rope and with muscles made of water, did not move away.

"Who," he began, disturbingly quietly, "are you?"

***

# Also by H. L. Macfarlane

## Fairy Tale shared universe:

**Bright Spear Trilogy**

Prince of Foxes

Lord of Horses

King of Forever

**Dark Spear Duology**

Son of Silver (Coming 2023)

Heir of Gold (Coming 2023)

All I Want for Christmas is a Faerie Assassin?!

**Chronicles of Curses**

Big, Bad Mister Wolfe

Snowstorm King

The Tower Without a Door

## Other books:

**Gold and Silver Duology**

Intended

Revival (release date TBC)

**Monsters Trilogy**

Invisible Monsters

Insatiable Monsters (Coming October 2022)

Invincible Monsters (Coming 2023)

The Boy from the Sea

The Unbalanced Equation (Coming September 2022)

**Short Stories**

The Snowdrop (part of Once Upon a Winter: A Folk and Fairy Tale Anthology)

The Goat

The Boy Who Did Not Fit

# Acknowledgements

Snowstorm King was the literal reason I decided to write an entire series of fairy tale retellings. Originally Big, Bad Mister Wolfe was meant to be a one-off, but then I saw a beautiful book cover available for use by Beth Alvarez, and I fell in love. And thus Snowstorm King, and the Chronicles of Curses series, was born!

It was weird writing this book, since the idea and plot stemmed from an existing image rather than the image following the idea. It was certainly an interesting process. I had the flu when I was writing the first half of the book which definitely made me hate it for a while! But I love it now, I swear.

Kilian is horrible. I wish Elina went ahead and slapped him when they first met. This isn't the last you've seen of them (nor of Scarlett and Adrian!) so be sure to stick with the rest of the series to see when they pop up again.

My next fairy tale retelling is Rapunzel. I'm really, really looking forward to writing a ditzy, annoyingly optimistic heroine - it's not a character I would usually write.

This was supposed to be an acknowledgements section and all I've done is talk about what's next. As always I would like to thank my editor, Kirsty, and my partner, Jake. And my bunnies! But most of all I'd like to thank each and every one of you who decided to pick up a copy of Snowstorm King and read it to the end.

# About the Author

Hayley Louise Macfarlane hails from the very tiny hamlet of Balmaha on the shores of Loch Lomond in Scotland. After graduating with a PhD in molecular genetics she did a complete 180 and moved into writing fiction. Though she loves writing multiple genres (fantasy, romance, sci-fi, psychological fiction and horror so far!) she is most widely known for her Gothic, Scottish fairy tale, Prince of Foxes - book one of the Bright Spear trilogy.

You can follow her on Twitter at @HLMacfarlane.

www.ingramcontent.com/pod-product-compliance
Ingram Content Group UK Ltd.
Pitfield, Milton Keynes, MK11 3LW, UK
UKHW041953190726
13854UKWH00005B/1935

9 781916 016330